Praise for Rebecca Rowland

"Rowland gets under your skin, down to the frigid bone marrow with this creepy-as-hell winter horror. Everyone has secrets, and this book amps up the isolation, dread, and paranoia to remind us how vulnerable we really are. It's a chiller!"

— **Christopher Golden, *New York Times* bestselling author of *The Night Birds* and *Road of Bones***

"*Eminence Front* is a frightful tale of winter horror guaranteed to send icy shivers of fear creeping up your spine. Rebecca Rowland has crafted a disturbing story, filled with engaging characters, that will leave you chilled to the bone and begging for more."

— **Owl Goingback, Bram Stoker Award-winning author**

"Dark and turbulent, twisting horror at its finest; *Eminence Front* latches onto the reader, slowly, inexorably, filling one with fright and with admiration of author Rebecca Rowland's skill for crafting wicked tales."

— **Eric J. Guignard, multiple award-winning author, including *That Which Grows Wild* and *Doorways to the Deadeye***

"Tightly and meticulously plotted, *Eminence Front* blends the polyphonic character-focused horror of King with a genuinely chilling cosmic-horror presence. Rowland's writing is an absolute joy to read, and I highly recommend this deceptively short novel for anyone looking for a shivery page-turner in the winter months."

— Ally Wilkes, Bram Stoker Award-finalist of *All The White Spaces*

"In Rebecca Rowland's *Eminence Front*, bad weather makes people do even worse things, or so it seems. A haunting, claustrophobic glimpse into the apparently idyllic lives of some very damaged folks during an epic New England blizzard, where a single whisper can be enough to shatter their lives."

—John Palisano, Bram Stoker Award-winning author of *Requiem* and *Ghost Heart*

"With the precision of an ice-cold scalpel, Rowland carves out a blood-soaked, snow-covered diorama of a suburbia from hell. *Eminence Front* offers a fascinating new lore that will entangle Rowland's flawed characters in ways the reader won't see coming, all the while whispering haunted melodies of white-hot madness."

— Philip Fracassi, author of *Boys in the Valley* and *The Autumn Springs Retirement Home Massacre*

"Wicked, lusty, blood-soaked, and tense, Rebecca Rowland's *Eminence Front* is the claustrophobic tale of a blizzard that does something terrible to a neighborhood...and the people who do far worse to each other. A brisk, unsettling shocker!"

—Jonathan Janz, author of *Veil* and *Marla*

"Rebecca Rowland has created a cursed cold-front of a novel, equal parts enigmatic and unnerving, that seeps right into the reader's circulatory system. *Eminence Front* causes hypothermia, trust me. By the time you realize you've lost your senses, it'll be too late: You'll already have succumbed to Rowland's chilling tale."

— Clay McLeod Chapman, Bram Stoker Award-nominated author of *Kill Your Darling* and *Wake Up and Open Your Eyes*

"*Eminence Front* exposes the dark secrets of a northeastern town during a blizzard. Rowland expertly ratchets up the tension and dread with a well-drawn cast of characters as we discover the grim truth that these are the kinds of horrors that refuse to stay buried."

— Paul Tremblay, author of *Horror Movie* and *A Head Full of Ghosts*

"Rebecca Rowland really knows how to gradually torque up the creepy as evidenced by her new novel, *Eminence Front*. A few flakes, a few words, and before long, the characters—and the reader—are engulfed in a blizzard of terror. Unique imagination and engaging prose make this story, once begun, hard to put down."

—Jeffrey Ford, author of *A Natural History of Hell* and *Ahab's Return*

"There is nothing scarier than a silent evil, and Rebecca Rowland captures that perfectly in *Eminence Front*. She takes the mundane and makes it a total nightmare. Great story."

—V. Castro, Bram Stoker Award-nominated author of *Maria the Wanted*

"In Rebecca Rowland's *Eminence Front*, the residents of a New England neighborhood find themselves under assault by a malevolent force wrapped in a fierce winter storm. Rowland combines incisive character portraits with steadily escalating strangeness, simultaneously evoking the best of eighties-era blockbuster horror and the deep weirdness of its nineties-era successors. These characters inhabit lives filled with compromise and regret, with frustration and lust, until what is in the storm comes for them and reality bends and fractures. Tightly constructed, the novel accelerates toward a remarkable ending that only deepens its mystery."

—John Langan, author of *Lost in the Dark and Other Excursions*

Eminence Front

Eminence Front
Copyright © 2026 by Rebecca Rowland
Cover by Anthony Galatis
ISBN: 9781960988850 (paperback)

CLASH Books
Troy, NY
clashbooks.com
Distributed by Consortium
All rights reserved.

First Edition 2026
Printed in the United States of America.

For Ronald Malfi,

*who gave me a transfusion even before we realized
we were the same blood type*

Eminence Front

Rebecca Rowland

Eminence Front -

1 An act. A pose. A pretense. A show that is put on just long enough to win favor.

2 To exalt one's status as a morally intact person when the opposite is true.

Definitions.net (2024)

"And through the drifts the snowy clifts
Did send a dismal sheen:
Nor shapes of men nor beasts we ken—
The ice was all between.

The ice was here, the ice was there,
The ice was all around:
It cracked and growled, and roared and howled,
Like noises in a swound"

-Samuel Coleridge,
Rime of the Ancient Mariner (1798)

(1817)

(1828)

(1829)

(1834)

Excerpt from:

One Hundred Years of Weird Happenings in the Centennial State

Chapter 5
"The Blizzard of 1946"

Ice was everywhere. It dripped from the wooden slats on the fences, painted the untreated gravel that connected one town to the next, and hung from the snouts of the Hereford cattle standing immobile in the fields beyond the Aroya Ranch.

The livestock stood frozen in the winter diorama, their heads turned purposefully into the spray of the storm. The cows had broken free of their tie stalls and inexplicably wandered into the field as night fell. The frozen drizzle grew into dense white flakes, bleaching the ground within minutes, their hoof prints quickly disappearing beneath a heavy blanket. One by one, the animals lowed as the cold wind furiously slapped their backs, urging them forward. The herd inched along the grazing field, their intended destination just a milky fuzz in the distance.

There were 530 cattle in all, the largest ranch holding in the state. The storm fled from the heart of Wyoming, tripping and tumbling across the valley nestled tightly between Denver and the Kansas border until it eventually spilled its guts across the wide plains. Within twelve hours, the snow piled waist-high. Truck wheels became buried under the blizzard's waste; many vehicles were abandoned on roadsides as kind merchants offered shelter to wayward drivers.

At the Aroya Ranch, the night's atmosphere was more

flake than air. The cows' legs stiffened and lost nearly all feeling in the frozen undertow, but the herd moved on, eventually reaching the wired fencing and turning to follow it as it curved back toward the stanchion barn. They never made it there. By morning, the dense piling of snow scraped their bellies, then walled them in place. As the sky crept towards noon, the animals collapsed, one after another, the spontaneous mass of warm-blooded bodies issuing a nearly imperceptible puff of steam, then sinking into the still-growing white terrain.

The storm cleared by late afternoon. All told, four feet of snow accumulated on the ranch's land. Its final layer draped like a wide coroner's sheet over an acre of dead cattle, leaving the ranch hands to work in constant shifts, transporting as many of the frozen corpses as they could to train cars headed for market.

Superstitious butchers would not handle the remains, and the meat was sold at a discount.

What drove the animals to misadventure, no one could explain.

Chapter One

John Stephenson was the last person on Earth who still owned a cable television box; at least, it felt that way to John. Everyone he chatted with online talked about *streaming*: streaming news, streaming music, streaming movies. John still owned a DVD player. He selected what to watch by reading the rolling grid of televised shows on channel two, the one labeled Guide.

A single beam of sunlight cast a faint rectangular spotlight on the hardwood floor. John flopped backward onto the couch and pawed at the nearby remote control. As the television screen screamed to life, its volume inexplicably turned too loud for anyone's hearing ability, a shapely woman in a form-fitting red dress paced determinedly in front of a green-screened map of southern New England.

"A winter storm warning is in effect for northern Berkshire County, Franklin, Hampshire, and western Hampden Counties from 8 p.m. today until 1 p.m. Thursday," the woman explained. "Light to moderate snow is predicted to begin sometime after 10 p.m. and may transition into a wintry mix of snow and sleet on Wednesday evening but will return to snow by Thursday, as the storm dissipates—especially for areas south of the Massachusetts turnpike."

John stuck the edge of his index finger into his mouth and absentmindedly chewed a rogue cuticle. Windy McAlister was the woman's name, though John had always called her Windy Weather in his mind. A meteorologist named Windy. The bullshit stench was strong on that one. More likely, the woman's name was Jennifer or Katherine or something else as mild as Ivory soap, and she'd changed it for marquee appeal. Sometimes, John wondered if anyone's name on the television news was real, although he had to admit: if Wolf Blitzer's parents had the foresight to bestow that moniker onto their son, he tipped his hat to them.

"Snowfall accumulation will reach 18 to 26 inches in some spots, with higher elevations receiving a layer of ice," Windy continued, waving her arm along the map like a game show model accentuating the curves on a French door refrigerator. "There is still some uncertainty when it comes to how far north the mix line will begin. That will have a big impact on snowfall totals, so stay tuned today and tomorrow for regular updates as our radar tracks the storm."

John glanced outside. His half-reclining position restricted his view to the neighbor's house across the street and the sky above it. Since the morning, the sun had hidden itself behind a wall of gossamer clouds, casting everything below with a silvery filter.

Windy cleared her throat, and John focused his attention back on the screen. "Snowfall will gradually taper off Thursday morning and temperatures are predicted to rise by the afternoon, so expect flooding in low-lying areas over the weekend. However, temperatures today will hold around freezing until sundown, then drop steadily to the low 20s overnight. Winds will pick up by midnight with gusts of 35 to 45 miles per hour possible."

Movement flashed in the corner of John's eye. In the window at the far end of the room, the top of a brown baseball cap bobbed toward John's enclosed porch. The metal storm door opened with a screech, paused, then slammed shut again. The cap reversed direction and bobbed back toward the road and out of sight. His groceries had been delivered, John thought. Any storm-inspired milk and bread crisis, avoided. He did not jump up immediately to collect the freezer items and put them away. The cold would keep them for now.

Windy Weather's backdrop morphed into a roadmap with a number of the thickest lines outlined in red. Route 141, the narrow thruway traipsing over Mount Tom, the area's former ski attraction, and winding into the valley would be closed after seven o'clock. "Blizzard conditions are expected to begin around 3 a.m. with zero visibility continuing until sunrise," Windy warned. "Drivers are being advised to stay off the roads, at least until the storm lightens Wednesday afternoon."

John snatched the remote from his coffee table and pointed it at the screen with the intention of shutting it off when Windy turned her body abruptly and faced the camera. She seemed to be looking directly at John. "If at all possible, do not leave the safety of your home, especially when the snow is falling." John thought he saw a small grin peek from the side of her mouth after she said this, but he shrugged off the thought and clicked the power button, dissolving Windy and her brightly colored visual aids out of existence.

"Don't you worry about that," John said out loud. His voice hung uncomfortably in the silence of the empty house. He thought of picking up his cell phone and calling Louis under the guise of checking to see if he needed anything in preparation for the pending weather emergency, but that would be too transparent. Besides, what good would it do? What help could he offer him?

John hadn't left his house in more than five years, not even to walk into his own backyard. A snowstorm, no matter how massive, wasn't about to change that.

Chapter Two

Carol Bennett nearly dropped her laptop piled a foot high with graded work when she stumbled into the classroom a minute after the bell. She'd missed homeroom, but her students rarely showed up to that, anyway. They were seniors, and most of them drove their own cars—if they made it to school at all, especially when the weather was intemperate. A dip below sixty degrees or a drop of rainwater and many of them turned into the Wicked Witch of the West, melting back into their cozy beds until the skies cleared once more.

"Somebody's tardy," one of the students said upon her arrival, much too loudly for it to be considered a mumble. "Did you have *an emergency?*" It was a kid in the front row—Jakob, the one who spent an inordinate amount of time in the boys' room every period, occasionally returning reeking of freshly crushed skunk roadkill. More often than not, though, Carol suspected the kid was rubbing one out in a stall. When he wasn't sneering at her, Jakob was leering unabashedly at the quiet girl sitting two rows away from him. A few months earlier, Carol had caught the girl flashing a sly smile back at him, and as if in a trance, Jakob asked for a bathroom pass and disappeared for twenty minutes, returning only to collapse into an instantaneous nap on his desk. Carol almost left him snoring when he didn't immediately rouse at the dismissal bell.

Carol steeled herself to keep from snapping back at the kid. "Yes," she replied calmly. "I'm afraid it was." She wanted to tell her class the truth. *Yes, children,* she'd quietly explain, *when my alarm rang out at 6:30, I awoke to find my 75-year-old hearing impaired mother curled up beside the shed in the backyard.* She'd slap the desk as if setting up the punchline. *It was thirty-eight degrees out last night. Do you know what happens to the elderly when they are left in what's, essentially, a big outdoor refrigerator all night?*

This was what the pedagogy experts would have called *a teachable moment.*

At forty-six, Carol hadn't planned to be sharing a house with Rose, but the previous spring, after her father's funeral and one frightening incident where Rose had been found wandering in the park near her Boston brownstone in the middle of the night, Carol cleaned out the second bedroom of her Cape Cod style house in the suburbs and moved her mother into it. Two months later, she awoke to a strange sound floating through her open window, the tinkling of something rhythmically striking her chain link fence. Carol looked outside to see her mother pressing her stomach against the back corner of the backyard, looking out into the neighbor's vegetable garden, her legs continuing to move in a walking motion despite her knees rotely slapping the edge of the metal boundary. Carol wrapped a robe around herself and rushed out to retrieve her confused parent, a life-sized battery-powered bunny marching interminably in place even as the gears inside her ground themselves to dust.

It had taken Carol a full hour to coax Rose to her feet, ease her back inside, and tuck her into bed. Luckily, Rose only seemed to wander at night; for most of the day, her mother was lucid and coherent, though Carol was careful to unplug the electric oven before she left for work each weekday.

Carol wasn't in her twenties anymore. She couldn't carry her mother like her father had often done when he was feeling playful. He had died with a full head of jet-black hair on his head. Carol's hair wasn't even gray but pure white. Over the course of nine months, she'd sprouted purplish hollows beneath her eyes and wrinkles alongside her mouth and temples. After the incident at the fence, she nailed slide locks along the top frame of almost every exterior door. Now, she had to transform into a ballet dancer, standing en pointe to unlatch the lock almost every time she wished to exit her own home. She grew tired just thinking of it.

"Maybe I'll have an *emergency* next time we have this class first period," another of her students muttered under his breath.

"Or next time we have a quiz," added Jakob in solidarity.

You do that, kid, she thought back. *Just remember to clean that jizz off the back of the stall wall before you leave.* She smiled innocuously at both children, then scanned her eyes over her plan book, completely forgetting what lesson she had begun the day before. She had penciled in a pop quiz on the Oregon Trail. She had hoped the kids would read the week's chapter. She hated standing in front of them, droning on in dry lecture mode. "Let's talk about Westward Expansion," she announced brightly. "Somebody tell me: what surprised you about the pioneers' experience? Or, what had you known about the Oregon Trail that was confirmed in the reading?" Carol scanned the sea of students. Most of them looked sleepy; a few bent their heads, furiously tapping on the cell phones resting in their laps.

Carol snapped on the document projector and slid a piece of lined paper beneath it. She pawed at her blazer pockets until she located a pen, then clicked it open and began to jot down notes as she spoke. "Let's talk about some of the hardships encountered by pioneers headed west." She wrote the word HARDSHIPS in capital letters, then looked up and scanned her class again. "Charlie, name one obstacle they encountered."

A tall, thin boy in the back row shook his head slightly as if to rouse himself. "Uh...sickness?"

"Yes," Carol nodded. "That's one thing." She wrote *disease* on the paper. "Denise?"

A light-skinned girl wearing a men's white tank under-shirt under an unbuttoned flannel shirt smirked at her. "They ran out of food," she said.

Carol wrote *lack of food* on the paper. "What's more troubling than having no food? How long can you go without food? Brayden?"

A kid slumped in his seat in the first row ducked slightly lower as if dodging her question. She stared at him, keeping a pleasant smile on her face.

"A couple of months," Brayden finally replied. "As long as you have water."

"Ah!" Carol responded, writing *access to drinking water for people & animals.*

"Indian attacks," yelled Jakob suddenly.

Carol wrote *attacks from indigenous tribes.*

"Cannibalism," yelled another student.

Carol made a slash next to *lack of food* and added *cannibalism?* beside it.

"Rattlesnakes," offered another student.

As Carol added this to the list, the girl sitting closest to the door stopped reapplying her lip gloss and frowned. "Cannibalism? Miss, there were cannibals on the Oregon Trail?"

Brayden rolled his eyes. "Yes, stupid. The Donner party? They fucking ate each other."

Carol started to caution her student about his language when Jaymen, the boy sitting next to him, broke in. "Not all of them. Only like, half of the ones who survived ate the dead people."

Carol nodded. "Yes, that's true."

The girl by the door hadn't closed her lip gloss but motioned with the applicator at Carol. "Why didn't they just hunt for food?"

"Well—" Carol began.

"Duh. It was winter," Lizzy, a pink-haired girl in the back row suddenly interjected. "It wasn't like animals were just walking all over the place, ready to be shot." She shrugged. "Shit: they were probably too cold to go out and find food."

"You're not wrong," Carol said. "You saw that excerpt from Patrick Breen's diary in the reading: their group experienced snow beginning in October, and they were hit with storms nearly constantly from December through March." She scanned the faces of her students; all were watching her with morbid fascination. Even Jakob had forgotten to sneer at her and instead appeared genuinely interested in what she had to say.

"Although most of the pioneers who perished died of starvation," she continued, "the second leading cause of death was exposure, hypothermia." She wrote *weather/snow* at the bottom of the list. "In some cases, the storms became the catalyst for the starvation: some of the travelers lost their main source of food when their livestock became buried in several feet of snow." She added the word *lost* to her last notation.

At this, multiple students began to talk at once, most of them engaging in side conversations about who would eat who should any of them be trapped in a blizzard on the wagon train going west. Carol regained control of the reins and instructed the students to break into their small groups to tackle an activity on The Treaty of Guadalupe Hidalgo.

Carol walked from cluster to cluster, nudging her students back on task when they drifted onto tangents, then stopped briefly at the wide window at the back of the room. Her perspective from her classroom on the second floor had remained relatively unchanged over the past twenty years. She had a bird's eye view of the busy road that snaked along the side of the school building, and she often spied children making the valiant attempt to dodge the truancy officers by sprinting across the narrow highway to the gas station and drive-thru coffee shop stationed there. Today, however, her eyes fixed on the sky.

It had been cold for weeks, the dismal weather typical of southern New England reporting for duty promptly following Christmas and angling to set up shop until at least mid-March. For the next three months, the sun would do business as a deadbeat dad, appearing randomly and only for brief periods of time; most days, everything above the tree-tops was trapped perpetually behind a wall of frigid haze. Now, however, the sky appeared as hoary silver, delicate striations of pearly slate like the heart of a gray agate stone, low storm clouds hovering close to the earth like ghosts.

When the bell sounded for the end of the period, her students clamored to return their desks into rows and scampered out of the door in a frenzy. Carol walked quickly around the room, adjusting desks to their original configuration, then returned to the table with the document projector to replace her notes with a clean sheet of paper for the next class. In their tumultuous exit, the students had jostled her notes, and the Westward Expansion lecture pieces had slid almost out of range of the camera. On the SmartBoard's broad screen, only her last notation could be seen:

weather/snow lost

* * *

The office belonging to Carol's department chairperson was sandwiched awkwardly between two classrooms, its sole entrance located in the middle of one while its only window looked out onto the other. David had applied a frosted overlay to the window for privacy and discouraged staff from visiting while a class was being held, but Carol slipped inside quietly before the bell rang to begin last period.

"Hey, sorry—this was my only free time today," she whispered, shutting the door behind her. "Your email said you needed to see me." Her eyes drifted around the tiny room. It measured perhaps five by ten feet in size, but David had managed to squeeze a desk, chair, and small loveseat inside, not to mention a dorm fridge that he kept stocked solely for his History department staff.

He leaned down to open the fridge's door as Carol sat down hard on the loveseat. "Water? Diet Coke? THC-infused seltzer?"

Carol sniffed. A waft of something musky had expelled from the cushions when she landed. Rumors circulated that David was sleeping with one of the teachers in the English department. Carol didn't much care either way, but the thought of their dried bodily fluids rubbing along her suit pants made her slightly nauseated. "No, I'm all set, though good to know about the seltzer for midterms week." Her eyes scanned the barrage of pictures and papers tacked to his walls. There were a few brightly colored drawings of mysterious figures and objects, likely composed by his preschool-aged daughter. Next to those, a row of snapshots featuring David as the main subject presented itself like a photographer's thematic series on exhibition at a museum. David with the dog. David with the wife. David with an ice cream cone. David with a soccer ball.

"How's everything?" David asked. "Classes good?"

Carol nodded. "Yeah, everything is fine." She continued to examine the walls. David feeding a giraffe at the zoo. David with daughter on shoulders. David wearing a chef's hat. Every shot was framed perfectly, David beaming an oversized, toothy grin at the camera each time. *If he ever goes missing, we are all set for flyer headshots*, she thought morbidly.

David tapped his pen against the faux leather edge of the desk blotter. "I have to start making the schedule for next year," he said, "so I'm checking in with everyone to see if they'd like any changes."

Carol frowned. "It's January. You're making the schedule now?"

David smiled, raised his eyebrows, and looked down at his hands. "Truth?" He paused, exhaling slowly. "No. But that's what I am supposed to tell you when I broach the subject of your excessive absences this semester." He looked at Carol. "You've been out a lot, and admin is getting antsy. You know how it is: when a teacher plans to quit, they run through their sick time." He flashed her an apologetic smile. "I feel like an asshole. They sent me to feel out what's going on."

Carol crossed her legs and folded her hands in her lap. "I've been here forever, Dave. Even longer than you," she said. "I've saved up almost two whole years of comp time. If I were planning to leave, I'd have faked an injury and milked that bank for months, headed to the Caribbean for a vacation or two."

David sat back dramatically and pointed at her with both hands. "That's what I said," he joked. "I told Tricia, Carol's not planning to quit. I have an alternate theory."

"Oh, yeah?" Carol said, laughing. "What was your explanation, then, pray tell? A plague of virulent herpes breakouts? Wicked drug problem?"

"So close," said David. "I said both."

They both chuckled.

David leaned back in his chair and looked slowly around the small room. "Sometimes I wish I had a window in here," he said. "It feels like a nuclear bomb shelter."

"You're not missing anything," said Carol. "It's gray out there. Gray, gray, and more gray."

"And the cold." David made a face of revulsion. "It's nestled its way into my bones. My marrow has frostbite."

Carol thought of her mother, curled up on the icy ground, her shallow breath coming out in faint white puffs. "The sky definitely says snow. I don't think we'll have school tomorrow."

"Or the day after," David added quickly. "It's supposed to storm into the evening. You know how the city is. We'll be lucky if we're plowed out by Thursday."

"Thank Christ I bought milk and bread," Carol droned facetiously.

"It won't last. You know how New England is. We'll probably get a rainstorm over the weekend, something that washes it all away."

"And floods the lower valley. We can't win."

The two were silent for a beat.

David smiled at Carol again. "Are you okay?" he said. "Really." He lowered his voice to a conspiratorial tone. "Don't quit on me. They'll make me hire that student teacher who's shadowing Rick."

"The one who's always annoyingly happy?" Carol asked. "Will she be bringing pom-poms to faculty meetings?"

"She's a ball of energy," David agreed.

"She's twelve," Carol drolled.

David rolled his eyes. "Rick can't say enough great things about her, but you know what's likely going on," he said, then paused for Carol's response. When she only shook her head, he added, "She's a cake pop."

Carol frowned. "A cake pop? What does that mean?"

David tapped his pen again. "You know, she's sweet, fun for parties, but when it comes down to it, her nutritional value is pretty much nil."

"She did ask me in the teachers' lounge last week if Antarctica was considered a state," Carol agreed.

"A state of what?" David groaned.

Carol pretended to consider this. "Cake pops have always grossed me out," she said finally. "All I can imagine is someone's dirty hands squishing broken cake into frosting and rolling it around in their palms."

"Seems slightly fetishy," David said. "And when it comes to his pert little acolyte, I'm sure Rick has thought about *that* quite extensively, too." He exhaled loudly. "So, returning to what I was saying: please don't quit. I don't think I can take another year of that girl. Or Rick panting over her."

Carol sighed. "It's my mother," she answered flatly. "She's been sick, so I had her move in with me, and it's been...hard." There was Rose again, lying on her side against the shed, her gray eyes wide open, staring into nothing. Carol had shaken her—too hard, she knew, but Jesus, Rose had scared her half to death. When her mother was finally safe under the covers once more, her body no longer shivering, Carol had finally gotten Rose to look at her.

I'm sorry, Carol signed. *Mom, I have to go to work.*

Rose turned her head and looked at the window. Beads of condensation wetted the pane, and beyond it, the first hints of daylight were breaking through the trees. Rose made a fist with her hand and nodded it at Carol. *Yes.*

Carol moved back into her mother's line of sight. *Stay in bed, please. Stay warm. The weatherman says it's going to snow later.*

Rose looked at her daughter. *Yes*, she repeated. *I heard it.*

Carol frowned. *I heard it.* Her mother was mixing up

words again, but she didn't have time to decipher what Rose meant. She glanced at the digital clock on Rose's nightstand. The school building entrance bell would be ringing. *I have to go,* she signed quickly. *I will be home right after school. I promise.*

Rose held her gaze for a moment, then shifted her eyes to look at the window again.

Back in the office, David volleyed a sympathetic countenance. "I'm sorry to hear that," he said. "If you need to take a leave—"

"No," Carol said, a little too loudly. "No. I will work something out." She stood to leave, resting her hand on the door handle. "But thanks," she added.

David nodded. "And hey, Carol?" She turned to look at him. "Is that how cake pops are made, for real?" he asked.

"I'm afraid so," Carol deadpanned.

David smirked. "That's gross. You've ruined them for me, you know."

Carol slipped quietly into the classroom. "Then my job here is done, Dave," she whispered. She walked quickly out the door and down the hall to the teachers' lounge.

Excerpt from:

Autopsy Report

Department of Coroner
Hampden County, Massachusetts

January —, 20—

MANNER OF DEATH: Suicide
CAUSE OF DEATH: Exsanguination due to multiple
sharp force injuries to the lower and upper extremities

FINDINGS:
1. Generalized pallor and evidence of exsanguination
2. Multiple incised wounds of the upper and lower extremities consistent with self-infliction
3. Left radial artery slit lengthwise from wrist to inner elbow
4. Right radial artery slit lengthwise from lower portion of palm to center of left tricep
5. Right femoral vein slit lengthwise from mid-thigh to 2 inches below groin
6. Puncture wound in left femoral artery 3 inches below groin
7. Multiple injuries/superficial incised wounds on forearms and thighs

LABORATORY RESULTS:
TOXICOLOGY:

1. Blood:

a. Ethanol 50 mg/dL

b. Drugs: cocaine 330 ng/mL, cocaethylene 300 ng/mL, benzoylecgonine 4800 ng/mL

2. Urine: Positive for cocaine, cocaine metabolite (ecgonine methyl ester), and cocaethylene

3. Ocular fluid: ethanol 0.15/100 mL

EXTERNAL EXAMINATION:

The body is that of a well-developed, well-nourished ███ ███████████████████████████████ ███████████████████████████████ ████████████████ The sclerae and conjunctive are unremarkable, without evidence of petechial hemorrhages on either. Both upper and lower teeth are natural, without evidence of injury to the cheeks, lips, or gums.

There are no tattoos, deformities, or amputations. Abrasion and contusion present on lower left hip extending to upper left thigh measures 6 ⅜" x 4" and is brown-purple in color and appears antemortem.

Rigor mortis is fixed at the time of the autopsy examination (see form 1).

DESCRIPTION OF MULTIPLE INCISED WOUNDS:

There are three incised wounds of varying length on the extremities, one puncture wound 2 inches in depth, and eight superficial incised wounds (cuts) on the extremities.

1. This incised wound is located on the posterior side of the right hand and right forearm and extends past elbow 1" into upper arm. The wound measures 11 ⅝ inches in length. The edges are smooth, and depth of penetration is ¾" to 1 ⅛" inches and follows radial artery. Subsequent dissection discloses the wound path through the skin, subcutaneous tissue and muscle, radial artery, and lower portion of brachial artery.

2. This incised wound is located on the posterior side of the left forearm. The wound measures 7 ½ inches in length. The edges are smooth, and depth of penetration is ⅔ to 1 inch and follows radial artery. Subsequent dissection discloses the wound path through the skin, subcutaneous tissue and muscle, and radial artery.

3. This incised wound is located on the anterior side of the right thigh. The wound measures 5⅝". The edges are smooth, and depth of penetration is 1" to 1 ¾" and follows femoral vein. Fresh hemorrhage is noted when the wound path intersects femoral artery. Path extends through the skin, subcutaneous tissue and muscle, and femoral vein.

4. This puncture wound is located on the anterior side of the left thigh. The wound measures ¼" and the edges are smooth. Subsequent dissection discloses the wound path through the skin, subcutaneous tissue and muscle, and femoral artery.

DESCRIPTION OF ADDITIONAL INJURIES TO FOREARMS AND THIGHS:

Right forearm: (4)
There is a ⅝" incised wound of the volar surface 2" from the wrist. This incised wound cuts through the surface of the skin and dermis.
There is a ⅛" incised wound of the volar surface 2 ½" from the wrist. This incised wound cuts through the surface of the skin and dermis.
There is a ½" incised wound of the lateral surface 2 ⅝" from the wrist. This wound appears superficial.
There is a puncture abrasion at the antecubital fossa.

Left forearm: (2)
There is a ¾" incised wound of the volar surface 1" from the wrist. This incised wound cuts through the surface of the skin and dermis.
There is a ⅝" incised wound of the volar surface 4 ⅓" inches from the wrist. This incised wound cuts through the surface of the skin and dermis and hypodermis and into Flexor Carpi Radialis muscle.

Right thigh: (2)
There is a ⅜" superficial incised skin cut, diagonally oriented, on the upper portion of the anterior thigh, 2 ½" from the groin. This incised wound cuts through the surface of the skin.
There is a puncture abrasion ½" above the knee on the anterior thigh.

Left thigh: (1)
There is an abrasion and contusion beginning 5" from the groin and extending onto the lower hip. It measures 6 ⅜" x

4" and is brown-purple in color. Tissue analysis of area indicates macrophage cell infiltration, suggesting antemortem injury.

INTERNAL EXAMINATION:
(continues on next page)

Chapter Three

Days before she had taken off, Steve's wife had been plotting. Steve Kline knew this. He'd seen *Sleeping with the Enemy*; he knew that even the most docile of chicks could drum up the gumption to escape if cornered tightly enough.

They had been together for fifteen years, married for nine of them. He'd had plenty of girlfriends before her, but Brandee was special. She was the first girl who he truly loved, or at least, who he genuinely liked. Steve was willing to admit that perhaps he didn't have the capacity to love. He was a self-centered prick, though he'd never admit that to anyone, not even Brandee, and he had told her things he never thought he'd tell anyone.

They first met when she serendipitously stopped by his work with a few of her friends at the close of his day shift. Steve was only twenty-four and bartending at Whistler's, a local dive that sold overcooked pizza and crinkle fries and served primarily as a home base for a profitable cocaine dealing business rather than for any aspiration to collect positive Yelp reviews. He was washing dirty glasses and watching the clock, mentally counting the meager tips in his pocket and calculating if they would sustain his night out with his friends. He reckoned he might be able to stretch the cash to cover his bar tab if he didn't eat dinner.

She stood hesitantly between two barstools, clutching a handful of sweaty bills in both hands like a penitent's offering. Steve stopped loading the ancient dishwasher and wandered toward her. "What can I do ya for?" he asked.

Her eyes darted nervously over the bottles behind him. "Um...a round of kamikaze shots?" she said, her voice lilting into a question mark at the end of her request.

Steve studied her face. She wore makeup, the kind that women spackled on from their foreheads to the edge of their necks, smothering every millimeter of skin, but when she tilted her head downward, he could see a specter of freckles dotting her nose and cheeks: an unavoidable accessory, he assumed, for her auburn-colored hair. Even in the dim light, Steve knew the girl wasn't twenty-one. Hell, she might have still been in high school, a teenager on a rebellious streak playing hooky from Algebra homework. "You got an ID?" he asked, though truth be told, he did so to keep the conversation going more than out of any respect for the law.

A pink flush rose from behind the powdery foundation. "Er, no, I...I didn't drive here, so—" She turned and glanced apprehensively at her companions, who were laughing and chatting loudly at a nearby table.

Steve held a hand up, then leaned forward. He could smell her now, a sweet perfume like spun sugar from a carnival. "I'll serve you, but you gotta be straight with me," he said, an insistent urge swelling in his groin. The spontaneous fatherly tone was getting him off a bit. "How old are you *really*?"

She grinned at him then, a real smile, one men savored if they understood how rare such things were. "I'll be twenty-one in August," she said, her voice barely a whisper. She kept her eyes focused on Steve's, and he watched her pupils swell to engulf him.

Steve held her gaze for a long minute, then nodded and commenced with making the drinks. He assembled the battalion of heavy-handed liquor onto a waitress tray and offered it to the girl. "What's your name?" he asked, adding quickly, "To put on the tab?"

She smiled sheepishly. "Brandee, with a double e." She brought the shots to the table, then returned immediately with the empty tray, holding her own glass, still full, in one hand. "I have to ask," she said, handing the tray to Steve over the bar. "If you were going to serve me anyway, why did you ask how old I was?" She winked, then tossed the mouthful of liquor into the back of her throat, placing the empty glass upside down on the bar top, Marion Ravenwood-style.

A handful of inches above his appreciative grin, Steve's eyebrow raised. "Because there's a show at the casino next Friday, and you have to be eighteen to get in, Brandee with a double e."

Just a few weeks later, Steve shimmied into a monopoly of prime evening shifts after the previous lead bartender, a crotchety townie with a round belly and wiry white eyebrows that jutted out in every direction, wrapped his Nissan around a telephone pole on his drive home. Steve had found those brows to be horribly distracting, so the absence of them combined with the opportunity to snag prime tipping hours had been a win-win.

Dating Brandee was the cherry atop that sundae. She was built like a brick shithouse, as his dad liked to say: plentiful tits and ass rounding out an athletic build of milky-white skin. She liked to wrestle in bed, and sometimes, but only sometimes, Steve let her win. When he did, she straddled his torso, her thick thighs squeezing the sides of him like a vice while she rode him cowgirl-style, and Steve folded his arms behind his head and watched her nipples trace zigzags in the air as they bounced along.

Each autumn after they married, Steve and Brandee decided where they would vacation the following year, and for Christmas, they bought each other a gift to use on the upcoming trip. When they spent Saint Patrick's Day in Savannah among the city's green water fountains, he bought her a necklace with a green shamrock pendant. When they traveled to San Antonio to sit front row at a Spurs game, he bought her a pair of cowboy boots with heels so high, she stood nearly as tall as him.

On their third anniversary, Steve bought an oversized map of the United States and taped it to the wall in their kitchen. Each year following, he traced the route they traveled on their annual adventure with a red marker until the poster appeared as a robust circulatory system infusing each corner of the country with life.

The year she left, they had planned to go to Key West to watch the Hemingway look-alike contest in July, so he bought her a first edition of *The Sun Also Rises*. When she opened the box Christmas morning, she held the book for a long time, staring at the cover.

The next day, Brandee told Steve she had to be at work early. It wasn't until he climbed into the front seat of his rusting two-seater to leave for his evening shift that afternoon that he saw the note she left on his dashboard. The Hemingway book lay unopened on the passenger seat.

Boxing Day would forever be the date life sucker-punched Steve in the gut.

Steve had suspected his wife was unhappy. He had known, deep in his chest, she would leave him someday. Still, he hadn't stopped her, had he? Why would he? Seven months after she disappeared, he hopped on the plane headed for the Keys, not bothering to cancel her ticket in the hope that maybe, just maybe, she would be waiting there for him. She wasn't, and Steve spent the week alone in a mostly drunken stupor, attending the Papa contest in the hundred-degree heat and subsequently projectile vomiting a brown spray of whiskey and masticated key lime pie all over the white beard of one of the contestants.

* * *

Soon after the four-month waiting period following their divorce proceedings had expired, Steve sat at his neighbor Dan and Janet's dining room table, sipping his third gin and tonic in two hours and staring out into space, The Who's *Face Dances* playing on repeat on the stereo. Steve hummed along to "You Better You Bet," tapping his index finger along with the guitar's chord arpeggios.

"I'd fuck Pete Townshend," Steve announced suddenly. "I'd fuck Roger Daltrey." He stopped tapping and instead pointed into the air for emphasis. "I love this band so much, hell, I'd fuck Keith Moon."

Dan raised an eyebrow at him. "Keith Moon in the 70s, or Keith Moon now? Because the latter could get a bit messy."

"Mushy," added Janet.

Steve slammed his hand dramatically on the table. "Blasphemy." He looked around the couple's dining room. "He's probably haunting that flat in London with Cass Elliott. You gotta think: any place with that much death has got to be cursed."

"What about John Entwistle? He can't get in on the action?" asked Janet.

Dan laughed. "Nobody fucks the bass player, babe."

Steve raised both of his hands to his face and rubbed his eyes. "I could do with a little cursing. Liven things up. I'm all washed up, my friends."

"You gotta see this as a new beginning," Janet said,

turning the bottle of Bombay Sapphire completely upside down to top off her own drink, the lime wedge having fallen into the glass and bobbing raftless alongside a single, barely melted ice cube. "You're not even forty yet. You've got a ton of stuff to accomplish yet."

"I'm thirty-nine," said Steve. "So, tick-tock to that." They were all silent for a beat, then Steve grinned at her. He'd always liked Janet. She was a happy drunk, and unlike most of his friends' wives, she never gave him shit for overstaying his welcome at dinner parties or barbecues, something Steve did quite often at the Murphys' as they were only two houses down and across the street from his own home.

Janet placed the empty blue bottle on the table. "I don't know if you're aware of this, but you're smack in the middle of prime Gen XY dating age, my friend," she said. "Everyone is getting divorced at forty. It's practically a rite of passage."

Dan placed a hand on her back and rubbed it gently. "She's right, you know. Our generation fucked around in our twenties, got married and raised a few kids in our thirties, and now that those kids are steering into teen territory, it's back in the saddle, my friend."

Steve propped his elbow on the table and rested his head in his hand. "Oh, yeah?" he said. "Aren't the two of you a half-decade to fifty? You've lived together on this street as long as I have. When should I anticipate one of you riding off into the sunset, then?" He forced himself to not look at Janet as he said this, though he could feel her eyes on him.

Dan chuckled and folded his arms over his chest. "A, we don't have kids, and B, we never got married," he explained. "Two important distinctions that make a world of difference."

Noodle, the couple's Labradoodle, nudged Dan's hand as it draped over the arm of the chair. In response, Dan rustled the fur on the dog's head. "Isn't that right, Noods?" He stood up and stretched. "I'm going to take him out," he told Janet, then nodded at Steve. "He'll help you with dessert."

Steve smiled. "I will, you know," he said to Janet as Dan snatched the leash off a nearby hook and exited. When the shush of the storm door sounded, he added, "Need a bump?"

Janet grinned. "Fuck, yeah. I thought he'd never leave." She pushed the dinner plates aside and brushed the side of her hand along the table, clearing a wide, open space.

"Well, Jesus, I'm not Pablo Escobar, here," Steve said, pulling a small clear bag from his shirt pocket. "Got a pen? One with a cap."

Janet riffled through a drawer in the nearby sideboard. "I thought Jackie was the only author on this street." She handed him a sleek fountain pen.

Steve waved it away. "No, not a nice one. A drugstore brand, the kind with the plastic cap you can take off."

Janet shuffled the contents of the drawer again until her hand emerged with another writing utensil: this one with a battered white barrel and a blue cap that appeared somewhat gnawed.

Steve accepted it, glancing only briefly at the damage. "Noodle chew toy?" he asked.

"More likely Dan's choppers," she said. "Ex-smoker."

Steve removed the cap, then opened the top of the baggie. He dipped the protruding clip of the cap into the white powder, then brought the tiny pile to his nostril, covering the opposite side of his nose with his other hand. One quick snort and the substance disappeared as Steve blinked his eyes rapidly. He held out the bag and pen cap to Janet, who scooped a small amount of the cocaine onto the cap's end and mimicked Steve's actions.

"This was your tip?" Janet asked, scrunching her nose a bit and returning the implements to her neighbor.

"Yeah," Steve replied, "the dealer who comes in once a week: he doesn't bother giving me cash anymore." He paused to inhale another bump, this one in his other nostril. "Matter of fact, he doesn't bother to pay his tab anymore, just hands me bigger and bigger baggies."

"I guess drinks are on you," Janet said, snorting another scoop of powder. She resealed the bag, then recapped the pen just as the sound of the door and Noodle scampering across the hardwood floors echoed in the front hall. Steve tucked the bag back into his pocket and rose to help Janet, who had begun to gather the dinner plates into her arm, stacking the used silverware on top of the pile.

Steve was grasping the spent water glasses by their rims as Dan entered. "So," Dan said, wrapping the leash neatly around his meaty hand, "Dessert?"

"On it," Janet said quickly, then skirted around him and into the kitchen; Steve, the ebullient helper at her heels.

* * *

Two months later, as Steve lay naked, sprawled along the guest bed while Janet showered in her bathroom across the hall, he thought about that night, how he and Janet had fumbled with the cake, their bodies bubbling over with happy energy and wanting nothing less than to eat anything, never mind a thick brick of sugar and frosting. He had carried the small plates and forks into the dining room anyway while Janet produced an obnoxiously large Santoku knife from the silverware drawer, holding it first over her head like a samurai then making an exaggerated show of cutting the most generous piece for herself. She spent the next half hour chopping and mashing it into pulp, grinning like the canary-swallowing cat while Dan pontificated about the Patriots' chances for another Super Bowl visit, completely oblivious to what had transpired.

They slept together for the first time the very next week.

It was the day Janet appeared on his doorstep, holding a

rectangular tray containing a generous meal of Thanksgiving leftovers. "Don't lie and tell me you ate a decent meal at Whistler's last night," she said, her breath white puffs of fog as she pushed the heavy glass receptacle toward him. She was dressed for the weather: a long, beige coat extending down her calves and a bright green scarf wrapped tightly around her neck.

Steve scratched the stubble on his cheek, then accepted the offering, his hands dipping a bit as he took on the surprising weight. "What did you make? This is hefty." He pulled back the aluminum foil top and peeked inside. A salty scent of bread stuffing mingling with seasoned turkey and other assorted delectables wafted upward, making his mouth water. He nodded at Janet. "Thank you: really. Hey, come inside. It's nipply as hell out here."

She followed him into the front hall, shutting the door tight behind her. They walked to the kitchen, and Steve opened his refrigerator to place the plate inside, then scanned the shelves' contents for something decent to offer his guest. "I have some ginger ale, and…orange juice? Beer, if you'd like one?" he said without turning around. "What can I get you?"

"Nothing," Janet said. Her eyes drifted over the map of Steve and Brandee's adventures covering most of the wall nearest to her. The red marker lines throbbed with painful memories, though perhaps they were still happy ones in Steve's mind when he stared blankly at the canvas each morning, sipping his breakfast coffee. "Really, Steve," she said softly, forcing herself to look away from the map. "I was just thinking of you and thought you might be hungry. It was just Dan and I yesterday, so there was plenty to set aside."

Steve shut the door and turned back to her. "Well, I am more appreciative than you know."

The two locked eyes for a long minute, then Janet began to unwrap the scarf from her neck. Without breaking eye contact, she unbuttoned her coat and let it fall to the floor. Only then did Steve take his eyes from hers: they raced downward, taking her all in. Janet was standing in the middle of his kitchen in only a bra and panties.

"If you think you'll like the dinner," Janet said, a grin growing wider across her face with each passing second, "just wait until you see what else I've brought you."

It surprised Steve to find that indeed, bending her over his kitchen table and fucking her was exactly how he'd been imagining it each night he returned home from one of their neighborly dinner parties. She wrapped her legs around his torso and her arms around his neck and shoulders like a spider monkey, and she wanted him just as badly as he wanted her. They spent the rest of the afternoon in his bed, and when he reheated the generous plate of food hours later, the two of them shared a fork then had sex all over again, their hands and mouths greasy and primal.

"This is going to be complicated, isn't it?" he asked as she finally got dressed, tying her hair messily into a makeshift ponytail at the top of her head. He silently chided himself as soon as the words had spilled from his mouth. It was presumptuous to think there would ever be a repeat of what had occurred between them. They were neighbors, for Christ's sake. And Dan was his friend. Wasn't he?

She leaned close to him, resting her forehead against his, then ran her hand along his cheek. "I think it's going to be easy as hell, actually," she said. "See you for dinner tomorrow night? Dan's making sausage and peppers." She kissed him, and Steve could still taste the sex on her tongue. He hoped she planned to shower before Dan came home, but a part of him, deep inside, also hoped that she didn't.

They remained in a strange limbo for the next two months: the three in their weekly get-togethers, the two in their semi-regular romp, first exclusively in Steve's home, then occasionally in Janet's. Once, when Dan made a spontaneous run to the liquor store to replenish their rapidly dwindling gin, Janet pushed Steve into her master bathroom, ripped down his jeans and boxer shorts, and took him greedily while Noodle sat in the doorway, watching the two of them in what Steve could only interpret as canine confusion.

Sometimes, they got high before they fooled around, but mostly, Steve and Janet had sex stone-cold sober, and it was for this reason that Steve began to believe that something beyond just an impetuous fling was happening between them. He trusted Janet. He liked her. He believed her.

Specifically, he believed her when she told him that there was no way Dan would come home early, so as he lay on her guest bed and heard a car outside pull up and shut off its engine, he wasn't concerned. Dan worked second shift as an administrator at the prison three towns over; he couldn't leave halfway through his shift, and Steve couldn't fathom an emergency that would warrant his neighbor being released from work.

When the muffled clatter of a key in the lock and the back door opening sounded from two rooms away, however, Steve's heart hitch-kicked into his throat. He rolled off the bed, collecting scattered pieces of clothing from the floor and frantically dressing in a streetlamp's hazy illumination from the nearby window. He glanced outside. Sure enough, Dan's truck was there, parked at the bottom of the driveway, its hot engine ticking like a metronome in the empty silence of the cold night air.

He shoved his feet into his sneakers, realizing a moment later that each was on the wrong foot. When he righted them at last, he patted the pockets of his jeans, making certain that he still had his wallet and keys. There wasn't time to button his flannel shirt, and he hadn't brought a jacket despite the freezing temperatures, but this was not the occasion to scold himself about it. As Dan's footsteps pattered about the kitchen and dining room just a few yards away, Steve cautiously but quickly unhitched the lock on the window, slid the pane upwards, and, sending a silent bit of gratitude into the universe that there was no screen, climbed carefully out and into the frigid evening. He stood on tiptoes to pull the window shut, then crept, Scooby-Doo-style, along the side of the house until he reached the sidewalk.

Steve's heart pounded in his chest, the adrenaline screaming for release in every nerve ending of his body. There was still a chance that Dan could look outside and see him wandering away from the house, so Steve broke into a quick jog, bounding across the street without checking for traffic.

The salt-smattered black Subaru swerved and screeched to a halt, its left headlight scolding him with a bump to his thigh as he sprinted in front of the car. Steve did not stop. He kept his eyes fixed on his front door, pulling his keys from his front pocket as he ran.

Chapter Four

She was certain she had hit him.

On the short route back from Whistler's Bar, Jackie did her best to drive without swerving. It was only four blocks, much of it industrial buildings that closed by five, so the streets were relatively empty.

It had still been daytime when she ventured out to the grocery store after the local television news shifted into a full-blown panic appeal, warning viewers to stock up on staples in preparation for the incoming weather. Sure enough, the shelves were a jumbled mess when she perused the aisles of the nearby A&P, but she carefully selected a handful of canned soups, pet food, and paper products. What remained of the bread was squashed or pummeled, so she doubled back to the cereals and dumped a few boxes of flavored instant oatmeal into her basket before heading for the check-out line.

Nothing was perishable, she rationalized as her car approached the purple sign for the local dive bar. She could park, go inside for a quick drink and maybe a slice of pizza, then be well on her way long before the storm began. Who knew how long the roads would be a slushy mess: on the last snowfall, it had taken the city over a day to send a plow to their street. Working from home afforded her the luxury of avoiding slick travel, but it was also claustrophobia-inducing. She made a concerted effort to get out and into the world at least once a week, mostly out of fear she might end up like John, her agoraphobic neighbor.

A beer buzz always felt different to Jackie than the one hard liquor brought forth. After three Allagash Whites, her body took on a cocooned feeling: she felt unusually warm, swaddled in a soft blanket. She knew she should not have ordered a fourth, and now—good Lord, she could have killed someone.

The man who walked in front of her car had come out of nowhere, or maybe she had been too busy fiddling with the garage door button to notice him. She slammed on her brakes, but there was an unmistakable bump that told Jackie she had hit him, at least tapped his body with her front bumper as he strode by. She couldn't have hit him too hard, though: he hadn't broken his pace but even sped up and began to run.

The man's hands jangled along the tops of his thighs, nervously strumming an invisible guitar string: a tell-tale sign of a junkie, Jackie thought, or maybe just a lifelong self-medicator who was an hour away from dropping into a sidesaddle jig along the floor. To make matters worse, this individual was walking around her neighborhood, skulking about just a few houses down from hers. It wasn't until he had safely touched his toe to the tree belt that Jackie realized: the twitchy pedestrian was her next-door neighbor.

She hadn't been far off in her assessment: Steve's intoxication habits were infamous on the street; they made her own problem drinking seem like child's play, especially after his wife hit the road the previous winter. Sure, he hooked her up with a gram or two of coke when she stopped by Whistler's during stints of writer's block (I mean, King did it, right? So what was the harm, really?), and yet, here he was, roaming the street alone after dark, bare-chested when it was below freezing outside.

She liked Steve. Hell, everyone did, and all of the residents on the street were decent neighbors: no one leaving oversized household items on their tree belts for weeks for the garbage collectors to ignore or blaring bass-heavy music exactly when she slipped under the covers for bed. Steve and his wife had lived next door for a decade, and they had been pleasant enough—certainly more social than John, who lived in the tidy brick Cape on the other side of her, a man she only saw briefly when he ventured onto his enclosed porch to fetch one of his frequent deliveries.

It was a quiet street: no excessive noise, no gossip-worthy drama. A staid neighborhood vacant of fodder for fiction.

Jack Mayr was her pen name, a sobriquet selected more out of spite than any passion for the moniker. Her birth name was Jacqueline Ketchum, but Dallas Mayr had absconded with the masculine version of that long before she had come on the horror fiction scene. It was her agent Billy's idea for the eventual nom de plume.

"It's tit for tat," Billy said, an audible slurp of caffeine echoing through the phone's speaker. Jackie didn't need to see him to know what was in the cup. If it was before five o'clock, it was coffee: black. Only after dinner should a respectable person indulge in alcohol in this business, he sternly declared at their first in-person meeting.

"If we're going to be punchy," Jackie responded, "I might as well go with Rita Slayworth. Or Jean Cleaver." She dumped two cubes into a rocks glass, unscrewed the top of a nip of vodka, and emptied the contents over the ice. It was four-fifteen. *Fuck off, Billy. Close enough.*

"Don't be an ass," said Billy. "Let's think long-term. This is your career we're talking about." And a semi-decent career it had turned out to be. After grinding through a decade of ghostwriting memoirs and nonfiction nonsense, Jackie finally landed a three-book deal with a big New York imprint at the ripe old age of thirty-one, and she'd been churning out a book a year under her own name, or at least, as Jack Mayr, ever since.

* * *

Most of the time, Jackie began work on the next title as soon as the previous one had finished final edits, but this year had been a tough one. Celebrating her fortieth alone had been an exercise in self-loathing topped with a splash of solidified substance abuse.

"Why didn't you tell me it was your birthday?" Steve asked, topping off her drink with a heavy sloosh of Tito's before pouring himself a shot and tipping it toward Jackie in salute.

"Why?" Jackie asked. It was August, and she had been sitting at Whistler's since six o'clock. Now, the last vestiges of sunlight were only purplish smatterings along the twilight sky. Her mouth felt loose, like the waist on a pair of jeans she'd worn without laundering one day too often. "You got a cake back there waiting? I'm partial to chocolate, if you're asking."

Steve dumped the alcohol into the back of his throat, then submerged the glass in the basin of soapy water in front of him. "You know what I mean, Jacks." He squinted at her. "The big four-oh and you don't have any big plans? You doing something this weekend, then?"

Jackie shook her head, embarrassed. "Nah," she said. "Might go out to the Cape for a few days, see my sister and the kids. Depends on the weather." It depended on whether her sister remembered her birthday and invited her down, but the admission seemed too pathetic to vocalize.

Steve agitated the glass about the basin, then placed it on

a rack in the nearby dishwasher. "Where's that guy you were in here with last week? Rick or Rob or Ron or something? What was his name again?"

He was trying to be folksy, but Jackie felt a wave of irritation, an overcompensation for her growing shame, rise in her chest. "Are you ordering us a set of monogrammed towels?"

"Are you trying to be a dick?" Steve retorted. He raised an eyebrow at her.

She bit her lip. "I'm sorry," she said finally. "I guess this is the start of the curmudgeonly decade in my life. It sucks so far. How did *you* deal with turning forty?"

Steve whipped his bar towel over his arm jauntily. "I'll have you know, madam, that I am still a spry thirty-nine, despite my meticulously manicured appearance." He smiled then, the edges of his mouth deepening the wrinkles scattered about his sun-weathered complexion.

Jackie smiled back. "Wow, I *am* a dick," she said.

Steve patted her arm sarcastically. "Yes, but you'll always be an older dick than me."

She raised her glass to him and drained it in three quick gulps.

* * *

It was five months later, and she was only halfway through her newest project, the one due to her editor in five days. She could squeeze him for a week or two extension, but the truth of the matter was, she had run out of steam. She had pitched the idea to Billy over Zoom when he was renegotiating her publisher's contract, Jackie sipping a heavy-handed Bloody Mary to nurse a throbbing hangover.

"It's a futuristic society where bankruptcy no longer exists. Those in debt must offer the healthy parts of their own bodies for society's lame and sick in repayment—"

"*Freejack* rewritten by Ishiguro?" Billy said, furiously jotting down notes on an unseen pad.

"The movie with Mick Jagger?" Jackie asked. "Didn't that movie bomb?"

Billy didn't look up. "It wouldn't have had Ishiguro penned the screenplay." He continued to write. "Keep going."

Jackie surreptitiously moved her hand to the back of her head, trying to rub the pain away. Earlier that year at a convention, she'd slept with another writer, the two of them emptying the hotel bar's last bottle of Macallan Scotch then retiring to his room under the guise of her retrieving a galley of his upcoming release. She awoke the next day, dry-mouthed and nauseous, but the man placed his hands firmly in the same place on her head, rubbing the occipital nerves until her muscles relaxed and the pain subsided. "You're a genius," she told him before exiting to shower in her own room.

"If that's your blurb, I'll take it," he said, handing her a copy of the previously promised book.

Jackie glanced at it, shoved atop a few other acquisitions on a dusty ledge of her bookshelf. She hadn't even cracked the cover.

"One character pulls a Willie Loman of sorts," Jackie continued. "The affluent throw underground dinner parties serving the flesh they've acquired from the poor. A real social commentary."

Billy looked into the camera at her. "On what? Equal access to health care? Economic disparity?"

"Yes, and yes," said Jackie. Who knew she was this good at bullshit on the fly? "I'm calling it *The Weight of Carrion Flesh*; you know, like that line from Shylock in *Merchant of Venice*: 'I rather choose to have weight of carrion flesh than to receive three thousand ducats.'" Jackie paused, watching Billy's face as it scrunched into the expression that communicated he was considering the proposal. She used the temporary recess to take another sip of her drink. It was thick on her tongue, the acid creeping hesitantly down her throat, unsure if it would be making a return trip since Jackie had neglected to eat breakfast again.

"I like it," Billy said finally, and jotted down a few more notes. "Dystopia is the cockroach of the literary world; interest in it will never die out completely."

A cluster of black pepper granules caught in her throat, forcing a cough. A spray of something bright red dotted the computer screen, and for a moment, Jackie forgot she had been drinking tomato juice and a checklist of respiratory cancer symptoms flashed across her brain. A soft nudge at her calf grounded her thoughts. Jimmy Changa, the fat orange cat who had shown up mysteriously on her doorstep the previous year, slid back and forth in front of her legs, demanding her attention. When she pushed him gently away with her foot, the tabby sprang at her shin, wrapping his thick, ginger-colored legs around her ankle and sinking his teeth into her Achilles tendon.

"Ow!" she cried, reaching down and shooing the cat away. "Fuck, that hurt!"

Billy was unfazed and seemed slightly relieved for an excuse to wrap things up. "House cats," he noted. "Low maintenance companions, but should you die in your house, take comfort in the fact that they'll eat your corpse before it even cools to room temperature."

"He greets me at the door every time I leave for more than an hour," insisted Jackie. "He likes me, I think. I mean, he *chose* to live here—how many pet owners can say that? He's just hungry right now."

Billy laughed. "Tell yourself what you need to," he said dryly, then signed off as Jackie's sad attempt at wiping the residue from her coughing fit only succeeded in creating crimson comet tails across her laptop screen.

* * *

Jackie pulled her car into the garage, then walked around to inspect the front bumper. In the dim overhead light, no damage could be seen, but Jackie was certain she'd hit Steve. It seemed odd he hadn't stopped, but maybe he was coked up. She'd certainly awoken to a barrage of bruises from an intoxicated adventure on occasion.

She grabbed the grocery bag from the back seat and walked to her front steps. The air outside felt thinner than usual. Jackie had lived in New England her whole life; this was typical for the calm before the storm. All day, she had sat at her writing desk and gazed outside at her barren backyard. The grass there was shriveled, curled into itself and nearly brown, with the occasional oversized pinecone scattered here and there. A gaunt squirrel dug at a piece of earth, found nothing, and scampered on his way. The sky itself was awash with a pearlish haze, Jackie remembered noting: the saddest Cheech and Chong movie ever.

Two doors down, a thin figure wavered just outside the doorway to her neighbor's house. Blanketed in shadow, whoever it was teetered slightly as if trying to find balance or perhaps just abounding in nervous energy. Jackie backed from her front steps and squinted to try to see who it was. When it slid quietly down the cement stairs and onto Carol's walkway, the streetlight's beam illuminated her face.

"Rose!" Jackie called out, waving her hand frantically in an overly enthusiastic manner. Jackie didn't know Carol and her elderly mother well. They might have spoken twenty words to each other the entire time they had lived on the street. Carol kept to herself, and from what Jackie saw, was an early riser. On weekends in fairer weather, she was on her hands and knees in her yard before seven, pruning her flower bushes and inspecting their leaves for aphids; on weekdays, she backed her car from her driveway by six and did not return until dinnertime. Teenagers from outside the neighborhood rode their bikes to her house every other week: in the summer to mow her lawn, in the fall to rake her leaves. The only time Carol made herself available to chatty passers-by was when a winter storm struck—she shoveled the sidewalk and path to her house herself, no matter how heavy or deep the snow. In those moments, Carol appeared vulnerable standing out in the open.

Jackie's semaphore arm caught the attention of Carol's mother, but the woman stopped only for a moment. The air was bitter cold—Rose's breath fogged lazily around her long white hair—but although she wore only a tattered nightgown, Rose did not shiver. Instead, she stared at Jackie for a long minute, as if trying to place her, then crept quietly to the tree belt, skulked about the shadows there, then doubled back around the far side of Carol's house and out of sight.

Jackie glanced back at Carol's house. No windows were alight. When Carol did not come outside, Jackie walked cautiously toward their house. Rose had walked along the side of the building shaded by a tall pine tree, and Jackie could not see anything past the edge of the first window shutter, but she continued on, holding her arms in front of her and willing her eyes to adjust to the darkness.

Pale moonlight bathed the backyard. Jackie had never been behind her neighbor's house and had only seen snippets of the yard from her own a few hundred feet away. The space was immaculate, without an errant branch or leaf marring the dormant lawn. In the back corner of the property stood a white-sided shed. Rose stood in front of it, her hand pressing against the door as if trying to push it open.

Jackie scooted around the opening in the chain link fence and walked slowly beside her. "Rose?" she said hesitantly. When the woman did not acknowledge her, Jackie repeated her call louder. When there was still no response, Jackie placed a hand gently on the woman's shoulder. "Rose, it's Jackie. From down the street." Rose's body felt angular, like a pile of wooden stakes beneath Jackie's hand. She continued to push against the shed door, increasing in force and speed until the metal structure seemed to give a bit and trembled against her action. "Rose!" Jackie yelled, her hand gripping the bony sheath of her neighbor tighter, "Rose, stop! Please!"

Carol appeared suddenly in Jackie's periphery, running awkwardly toward her mother while stripping her own bathrobe from around herself. She enveloped Rose in the terrycloth covering and Jackie pulled her hand away.

"I was just—" Jackie began, suddenly ashamed of having yelled.

Carol hugged the robe around her mother and turned the woman's body away from the shed. Rose kept her eyes fixed on the metal door, even as her body positioned itself in the opposite direction. "It's okay," Carol said to Jackie. "Thank you. Thank you for trying to help, but I've got it."

Jackie's hand dropped to her side. "I...okay...okay." She shoved her hands in her coat pockets and followed behind the two women until they reached the back of the house. Then, she walked to the top of the yard where the fence, apparently in place for ornamental reasons rather than to keep anything in or out, did not continue and exited to the driveway. She turned to look at the women. Rose appeared like a boxer before a match, the heavy robe draped over her shoulders as her hands jutted forward, moving insistently in a fixed pattern. Her lips did not move. Carol was nodding but kept her hands planted firmly on her mother's shoulders, guiding the elderly woman forward.

When they disappeared inside without a word, Jackie walked back to her own house and let herself inside, snatching the paper bag of groceries she'd abandoned at the bottom of her stairs. As she snapped on the table lamp in her living room, Jackie was momentarily startled by Jimmy

Changa sitting tall beside it, staring at her unmoving as she removed her coat and kicked off her boots. "You must be hungry," she said, pausing as if anticipating a response. "Alrighty," she continued, "I stocked up. No need to panic and start nibbling on the furniture, or your roommate." She reached hesitantly toward the cat's head and stroked it gently. "How was your afternoon? Mine? It was fine. Almost ran over one neighbor and caught another trying to break into her own shed, but otherwise, it's been uneventful." This was how the crazy cat lady stereotype must have come to be, she thought. Lonely, middle-aged women talking to their pets like human companions.

Was she lonely? Jackie considered this as she peeled open the top of a can of cat food and scraped the contents into Jimmy's bowl with a fork. The rest of the supermarket haul she stacked neatly in her kitchen cabinets. She allowed her eyes to hover over what she saw there. She had nothing to make a dinner for two: everything was single serving size except for a bottle of olive oil and an ancient box of macaroni and cheese. She ate when she was hungry with no regard for prescribed mealtimes, and more often than not, she ordered takeout, then surfed the wave of leftovers for days following. Her need for companionship aligned with her need for food: when she craved interaction, she went out and was social, often capturing the remnants—the cadence of conversation, topics discussed—and sealing them away in a glass jar to repurpose later in her writing.

Jimmy Changa finished his meal, scraped at the ground with one paw as if to bury his dirty dish, then made a 180 and walked past his owner without so much as a hint of gratitude.

No, she wasn't lonely, she decided. Jackie had learned to compartmentalize, and it was working, at least for now. She did wonder, however: with no partner, no best friend, no outside work environment to speak of, if she died in the house suddenly, how long would her body remain undis-covered?

Outside of her kitchen window, the world lay dark. Even the faint moonlight had put itself to bed. One white flake sailed idly past the pane, chased along by two more. Jackie opened her refrigerator, took out a half-empty bottle of Vinho Verde, and poured herself a heavy nightcap.

Transcript from:

Channel 7 News
Raw Footage

LANA HASTINGS: Are they ready?

WILEY ESTABROOK (off camera): Yeah, yeah. They (unintelligible) warm in the car. The blue Toyota over there.

LANA HASTINGS: Well, go get them. It's cold as hell out here. (unidentified rattling sound)

Dammit! Will someone close the tent? I just got snow all over my hair. Wiley, do I need makeup in here?

WILEY ESTABROOK (off camera): (unintelligible) (two minutes without dialogue passes)

LANA HASTINGS: Should you mic them? Maybe you should mic them. No? Okay. Make sure you get the spelling of their names right. No, double-check it.

WILEY ESTABROOK (off camera): We're rolling. Ready when you are.

LANA HASTINGS: Hi, Matt. (coughs) Wait, are we going live, or is this being edited in the studio? Never mind. I'm editing it. Starting again. (pause) Good evening. I'm standing with two students from Central High School, Elizabeth Smith and Jaymen Soto.

JAYMEN SOTO: J-A-Y-M-E-N-S-O-T-O

ELIZABETH SMITH: She doesn't need the spelling of your name *now*, dumbass.

JAYMEN SOTO: Oh.

LANA HASTINGS: It's fine. I will edit that out. (pause) Jaymen, you and Elizabeth don't live in this neighborhood, but you came here once a week throughout the fall. Can you tell me why?

JAYMEN SOTO: Yeah, I rake leaves for Ms. Bennett, my History teacher. I mean, I used to.

ELIZABETH SMITH: I mowed her lawn. She paid pretty good, too. I mean, she probably couldn't afford it, being a teacher and all, but she always paid us decent. And under the table.

JAYMEN SOTO: Dude, don't tell people that.

ELIZABETH SMITH: Right. Edit that out, too, okay?

LANA HASTINGS: Did you ever witness Ms. Bennett doing anything aggressive? Violent?

JAYMEN SOTO: Violent? No. No, never. I mean, she was strict and all, but—

ELIZABETH SMITH: She threw a pen at a kid once.

LANA HASTINGS: You witnessed Ms. Bennett throwing a pen at a student?

ELIZABETH SMITH: Well, no, but I heard she did once.

JAYMEN SOTO: Ms. Bennett was nice. Her tests were hard, and she made us read way too much. I liked her class, though.

LANA HASTINGS: Did she also hire you to shovel snow?

ELIZABETH SMITH: No, but we figured, once the roads were okay, we'd drive over and if her driveway wasn't plowed, we could offer to shovel her out. You know, make a little extra cash.

JAYMEN SOTO: Her sidewalk was kind of clear. You know, like someone had maybe started shoveling it before the storm was over. But her driveway definitely needed to be shoveled. It was still snowing a little, but not a lot. Like, it was going to be over in a few hours.

ELIZABETH SMITH: We kinda pushed through the snow to get to her side door—that's where she always stood when we came over in November—and we rang the bell, and...(unintelligible)

LANA HASTINGS: You went to her door and rang the doorbell, but she didn't answer.

JAYMEN SOTO: We could see her through the glass. It was...it was awful.

LANA HASTINGS: You saw Ms. Bennett through the window in the door?

JAYMEN SOTO: I...I don't know if that was her.

LANA HASTINGS: You don't know if the person you saw was your History teacher?

ELIZABETH SMITH: She was (unintelligible)

LANA HASTINGS: Say that again. What did you say?

(whispering heard in the background, content unintelligible)

LANA HASTINGS: Wiley? Wiley, get them out of here.

JAYMEN SOTO: Maybe it wasn't her. But that's what the woman who looked like her told us.

LANA HASTINGS: Woman who looked like who? Carol Bennett? Didn't you see Ms. Bennett?

ELIZABETH SMITH: She looked like her...but...she...she...she

LANA HASTINGS: Ms. Bennett was long dead by the time you arrived at the house. Her body was found in the garage, not in the kitchen. You must have seen someone else.

WILEY ESTABROOK (off camera): Kids, let's go.

ELIZABETH SMITH: I know what I saw. She... (crying)

JAYMEN SOTO: It was HER. Just not...*her*, you know? (whispering, unintelligible)

LANA HASTINGS: No. No I don't know what you're saying. What do you mean, it wasn't her? I—

WILEY ESTABROOK (off camera): Lana, where are you going? We have to shoot the outro.

LANA HASTINGS (off camera): (unintelligible)

WILEY ESTABROOK (off camera): Lana! No—wait—

(high-pitched scream heard off camera)

Chapter Five

Kim O'Dell lay in bed, staring at the bumps and ridges along their popcorn ceiling. An errant cobweb had somehow escaped her routine that morning, and Kim willed herself to stop looking at it. She would eradicate it in the morning. If she got up now and fetched the duster, it would only lead to more cleaning projects, and she promised Tom she would lie down and get some rest.

The light from his office was still on, the incessant *click click click* of the computer keyboard tapping like a telegraph in her ear. Outside, in the frigid darkness, a car's brakes screeched but no further sound followed.

"Are you coming to bed soon?" Kim called. Tom had been at his desk all day. He'd even missed dinner, which had thrown a wrench in their entire evening plans, one domino tipping the next. The boys had basketball practice, and Kim timed the slow cooker to be ready exactly fifteen minutes after they returned home. That left a half hour to eat, then a half hour to shower, and an hour for homework time. They waited ten minutes for Tom to join them at the dining room table. The electric cooker tread water in WARM mode as

Kim envisioned the edges of the casserole slowly drying out, turning brown, and sticking to the heavy porcelain walls of the interior dish in a crunchy mess. Finally, she handed Aaron the serving spoon and asked him to divvy out the meal while she investigated what was taking Tom so long in his office.

She found him with his cell phone pressed firmly against his ear, his eyes fixed on the computer screen. "Yes, yes," he said, the exasperation dripping in his tone, "the original file was corrupted, but I managed to salvage the data and piece it back together." He paused, his gaze drifting upward toward his wife. "I just want to run the numbers one more time to make sure we didn't miss anything. You'll have it in the morning. By nine at the latest." He rolled his eyes at Kim and made a *let's wrap it up* sign with his free hand.

Kim leaned against the door frame and waited patiently. Tom began working from home during the Covid-19 pandemic and never returned to the central office as his productivity scores logged surprisingly better while he toiled along in his own house. He only ventured to the company's headquarters once a month, and Kim liked being able to fix him a hot lunch. Moreover, she liked having a tighter grip on the family's schedule. She was no longer at the mercy of weather turns or traffic whims. She informed Tom when dinner would be ready, and Tom was there, at the table, just as the dish was removed from the oven.

Mostly.

Tom nodded as if the person on the other end of the call could see him. "Yes, yes, but—" he began. After a long pause, his voice resumed, having dropped a few notches in volume. "I understand. It will be done tonight." Kim opened her mouth to protest, and her husband held up a hand. "Yes, okay. I'll email you in a bit...Fine." He pulled the phone from his ear and tapped the red END on the screen. "I'm sorry, honey. I tried. I have to get this done."

"We have two teenage boys, Tom," Kim said. "If you want dinner, I suggest you take a quick break and at least come take a plate to go before it's in their stomachs. You know how it is: mealtime is survival of the fittest these days."

Tom looked back at the computer screen and tapped lightly on his keyboard. "I'll be down in a minute. Don't wait for me."

And the boys hadn't. When Kim returned to the table, they were shoveling spoonfuls of her casserole into their mouths, burnt edges and all. "This is good, Ma," the younger of the two, Dylan, garbled through a mouthful of masticated pasta.

Kim slid into her seat at one end of the table. Her sons had scooped a small ladleful onto her plate, a portion much smaller than theirs—a quarter, really—because they knew that Kim was watching her weight. She was always watching her weight. And the color of her teeth. And the shininess of her hair. And the length of her nails. Her eyebrows were perfectly angled because Kim spent the first fifteen minutes of every day plucking at them with tiny tweezers in a magnification mirror that made her pores appear as moon craters and the downy fluff on her cheeks a bearskin rug. She spent the fifteen minutes after that sloughing every inch of her body with a rough brush akin to the one with which Karen Silkwood had been scrubbed after testing positive for radiation (or, at least, the one Meryl Streep pretended to endure in the movie version). She didn't work out because women were supposed to be fragile and soft, but she did attend yoga class three times a week because women were supposed to be flexible.

Kim met Tom in her freshman year at Boston University. Her parents sent her to the school specifically to find a husband, one who could support her financially so that they didn't have to carry the burden themselves. Sure enough, the two were married the June following her junior year, and

Kim never returned to the school, happy to follow Tom across the country to cheer him on through his doctorate while dutifully downing birth control pills until he landed a six-figure salary at an insurance firm in Hartford, Connecticut. They bought a four-bedroom home in Western Massachusetts so that Tom could be close, but not too close, to his parents in Winchester, and a year after, Aaron was born. Dylan followed eighteen months later. Tom wanted to try for a third—a girl this time, perhaps?—but that would have left them with no guest room to speak of, Kim explained, and the layout of the house was so perfect as it was.

Kim worked for a short period, right at the beginning of Tom's graduate studies, but she had done so more out of claustrophobia in their tiny student housing apartment than out of financial need, and once they became homeowners, well, her job as a homemaker became a full-time one. Every day, Kim cleaned the bathrooms—all of them, with bleach. She alternated days between vacuuming and washing the floors, but she dusted every inch of the two-floor home every morning, spending the two to three hours between dropping the boys at school and fixing Tom's lunch carrying a spray bottle of Endust in one hand and a cotton cloth in another like a mercenary on assassination assignment.

Kim and Tom had lived in their home for sixteen years, and Kim happily snuggled next to her husband for almost every night of them, save a handful from when the boys were born, and of course, the weeks at the private facility Tom had encouraged her to attend a few years back, if only so that she could get back on track and be her best self for him and the children.

Tom's keyboard clicking was boring holes in her skull.

"Babe?" she called again. "You've been at it for hours without a break. Surely, he isn't checking his email at eleven at night." She looked down at her nightgown. She was wearing the red nightie, the lacy one that pushed her boobs into round melons below her bony collarbone, because Tom always told her he liked the look of her skin against it. The underwire dug into her torso, and as she lay there, staring at the cobweb despite her best efforts, she thought of the metal curvature piercing her lung, deflating it into a flattened pool of mush.

She heard his rise from his chair, the creak of the keyboard drawer closing, and Tom's muted footsteps as he padded barefoot across the carpet and into their bedroom. "I'm done," he announced. "Nothing more until the morning: I promise." He bent down to kiss her on the top of her forehead. "Let me take a quick shower, and I'm all yours."

Kim pasted a smile across her face. It remained there until she saw the door to the master bath shut and the sound of the shower running began. Tom would remain in the bathroom for fifteen to eighteen minutes, like clockwork. Kim liked that he was predictable. It made everything so much easier.

She slid from her space in the bed and wandered to the window. Outside, the moon hovered like a helicopter parent, its edges alight with a holographic glow, the halo Kim had seen occasionally in previous winters. Small handfuls of fat snowflakes drifted to the earth, sticking to the pavement in a pointillism array. More was sure to follow. The news predicted a major winter storm, and they were going to get one, she was certain.

Below, their next-door neighbor, Janet, was wrestling with her golden-colored dog on a leash. She stopped halfway down her driveway to zip her heavy jacket up to her neck. Despite having lived next to them for nearly two decades, Kim didn't know Janet or Dan well. They attended their barbecues, brought a bottle of wine to their annual Christmas Eve dinner each year, but she didn't think she'd exchanged more than cursory conversations with either of them. Tom and Dan were close, however, and often went out for beers at Whistler's, the local dive bar, and traipsed into the woods a few times each summer for hunting weekends, though Kim could not recall a time when either of them had returned with game.

The dog—she thought its name was Noodle, but she wasn't certain—was well-behaved and rarely barked. Kim was grateful for that. She was also glad that the couple kept the dog inside during outdoor festivities or hidden in a room during indoor ones. There was nothing more disgusting than a dog slobbering all over someone's hands or shaking its discarded fur over a visitor's pant leg or jacket. Pets were, quite frankly, a nightmare. Although the boys had begged them for a dog, a cat, even a caged rabbit, Kim had dug her heels in hard. She had her hands full keeping the house clean as it was with four humans residing within; add an animal, and the routine would never be done.

Kim watched Janet as the dog led her down to the sidewalk, sniffed briefly at the bushes at the end of their property, then continued up the street. His big paws left round smears in the freshly fallen snow, and Janet seemed to be taking great care to step into them and leave the rest of the white untouched. When they were two houses away, however, Janet stopped abruptly. Although the dog appeared to be pushing her to walk further, Janet stood fixed in place. She removed the knitted cap pushed over her head and craned her neck slightly as if straining to hear something in the distance. After a long moment, Janet knelt down and leaned her face close to the sidewalk. The dog, fascinated by his owner's proximity to him, nudged her head with his, but Janet pushed Noodle away and pressed her ear against the ground like a tracker listening for hoof beats. Curious, Kim listened, too, pressing her ear against the cold glass.

"What do you hear?" Tom asked, startling her. He rubbed his wet hair with a towel while walking naked toward the opposite side of the bed.

Kim pulled away from the pane and shut the blinds. "Nothing," she said quickly. "It's starting to snow," she added, then slipped back into place beneath the covers, trying desperately to rearrange the sheets as they had previously been draped. She looked down at her cleavage and, as her husband turned to hang his towel on the hook behind their door, surreptitiously reached inside the cups of the nightgown to push her nipples upward.

Tom folded back the bed covers to slide in next to his wife. He leaned on one arm atop a pillow and yawned, not bothering to cover his mouth.

Kim ran her hand slowly over Tom's shoulder and tricep, her fingers tracing the chiseled ridges of each muscle. He kept himself in good shape, Kim thought, and she was grateful for that. Most of her friends' husbands let themselves go after they turned thirty, soft paunches of belly swelling beneath tattered band t-shirts from concerts they'd attended in college. "You didn't eat dinner," she said.

"Nope," said Tom, a playful, bratty edge to his voice. "Totally slipped my mind."

"Want me to make you something?"

"Nope." Tom ducked away from her hand and gently pushed on his wife's shoulder to ease her backward. His eyes darted around her neck and torso. "I always liked you in this one," he said, touching a finger lightly to the strap on her nightgown.

Kim smiled. "I know."

Tom let his finger linger for a moment, then he returned his hand to the side of his head, propping himself against the pillow once more. "Give any more thought to what we talked about last night? The club?"

Kim had hoped Tom would forget, but she didn't allow the admission to register on her face. "I haven't. Not yet." She steeled herself to continue the discussion she had managed to duck the previous evening. "Where did you hear about this place again?"

Tom smiled. "A guy at work was telling me about it the last time I came into the office. He and his wife go about once a month."

"Really?" Kim said. "Wouldn't that be awkward, seeing a co-worker at a sex club?" She tried to imagine the place Tom had described: an old, semi-abandoned theater, complete with a balcony and velvet-upholstered chairs. The very thought of it, of the layers and layers of filth and grime coating the seats and carpet, made her nauseated, but she forced a small smile to peek around the edges of her mouth.

Tom returned his hand to her nightgown strap. "They open at noon every day and don't close until two in the morning. If we went in the afternoon, maybe on a day the boys are tied up until late, I doubt we would see anyone."

"Doesn't that defeat the purpose?" Kim asked.

"I mean, anyone we *know*," clarified Tom. He traced his finger along the edge of her collarbone, pausing at the top of her shoulder for a moment before running it back toward her cleavage. "You told me once that you love it when I show you off. I mean, this body—" His fingertips drifted to the top of her breasts and slowly traced each one. "This body is fucking dynamite, honey. Aren't you proud of it?"

She blushed a little at this. She worked hard to stay in shape, and admittedly, it felt good to have a husband who appreciated that. But did that mean she wanted to perform sex acts with him for an audience? "Taking an afternoon on a school day would mean I wouldn't have time to make dinner," Kim said. "You know how important that is to me."

"The boys are old enough to order a pizza," said Tom, "and the place has a buffet. Lunch and dinner. Late-night as well. There's really—"

"Wait—" Kim stopped him. "The sex club has a food buffet? They're serving platters of food while people are rolling around naked everywhere?" Kim tried to envision this arrangement. What did one serve at an orgy? Pasta seemed too filling. A salad bar, too provincial. Pigs in a blanket seemed too on the nose. Finger food, then? Steak-tips? Tiny quiches? Hot wings? The very thought of it made her wince.

"I guess," said Tom, shrugging. "Does it matter? You wouldn't eat it, anyway." He smiled, hoping to show his wife he was teasing her with the last remark. "Besides, *you're* the one I want to see on the menu." He leaned closer to her and began to kiss her shoulders and neck greedily, and she wrapped her arms around his shoulders in response. "Just thinking of you," Tom whispered into her ear, his breath hot and forceful. He continued to kiss her skin as he spoke. "Thinking of you, lying there, while other men consume you, all of them at once...it, *fuuuuuck*, Kimmy, it just—"

He moved on top of her as he said this, the excitement accelerating in him faster than Kim could catch up. She closed her eyes, feeling him wrench her panties down her thighs and his body push insistently against her. Kim tried to imagine what it would be like: naked, lying on a strange bed in a dimly lit room while strangers encircled her, touching her, her own husband watching hungrily from a few feet away. Strangers' hands. Strangers' naked bodies. The sweat from their armpits dripping on her, the oil on their faces rubbing onto her skin, the dirt under their fingernails inside her—

She pushed her hand hard against Tom's chest. "No, no —" she insisted, pushing against his weight. "Tom, no. I'm sorry. I can't. I can't right now."

Tom lifted his torso away from his wife and searched her face, confused. "What? What do you mean? I thought—"

Kim used this window of opportunity to slide out from under him. She scooted sideways to the edge of the bed and got out, her coltish legs momentarily tangled in the loop of panties around her knees. She simultaneously pulled them back up to her hips while sidling toward the door. "I have to use the bathroom," she said, not meeting her husband's eyes. "Give me a minute, okay?" Without waiting for a response, she walked onto the cold tiled floor and shut the door behind her.

Kim sat on the edge of the tub, bending her head toward her knees. She willed herself not to be sick. A deluge of thoughts flooded her head. She and Tom had a healthy sex life: a fulfilling one. His suggestion seemed to come out of nowhere. Kim did everything she could to keep Tom happy. That was what a wife's job was: to care for her husband. Wasn't it?

And yet.

Strangers. Sweat. Grime. Dirt. Disease. Infection. All of it tapped at the back of her gag reflex.

Her stomach lurched. She imagined the masticated casserole churning within her belly, springing on the trampoline positioned there, ready to sail back up her esophagus and into the porcelain sink, her immaculate sink that still smelled of chlorine.

Kim took a long, slow breath, pushing the air into her abdomen like they had taught her at the treatment center. She held it there for a long moment, then slowly released it. She stood up and glanced at the window. The heavy heat from the room was forming condensation on the cold glass. Kim wiped the wetness with the side of her hand and looked outside.

Janet and the dog were gone. Their footprints along the sidewalk were only faint apparitions. The neighborhood surrounding Kim's home slept silently beneath a steadily growing white shroud.

Chapter Six

Hot water sluiced over Steve Kline's face, the insistent spray of the shower pummeling his forehead until his eyelids pruned shut and his cheeks felt as hot and swollen as a tenderized steak. He sat naked in the tub with his knees bent, his head resting against the wall. The water had run for at least twenty minutes, and the tank was certain to exhaust itself soon, but he would wait until it was icy to move.

Dan must have known, Steve told himself. He must have known, and that was why he came home early, no call, no warning. He had intended to surprise them, and Steve had been surprised, all right. In fact, it wasn't until he was inside his own home again that he even had thought to warn Janet. He left her in the shower, unaware that her cuckolded husband had returned. He considered texting her, but that seemed the worst possible option. What if Dan picked up her phone? What if the screen were in eyeshot?

No, Janet would handle the skip in the record like a champ, Steve decided. At least, he hoped.

The radio on the top of his toilet was tuned to the local classic rock station, Allan Clarke of The Hollies crooning on about a tall lady in black. A gravel-throated deejay broke in with a station identification. Radio stations were like brick-and-mortar bookstores, Steve decided: twentieth century leftovers on their way to becoming ancient relics.

Not unlike himself, he thought.

At this, the first sizzle of a slow dance Bossa Nova beat echoed from the portable radio's speakers, followed by the tittering pulse of synthesizers. Steve rose to his feet, strumming his own stomach as an air guitar as The Who's signature riff signaling "Eminence Front" blared. An operatic carnival—that's what he used to tell Dan his favorite band's music resembled.

"When did The Who hire a hype man?" Dan responded each time.

Dan.

Fuck, Steve thought. *How can I look him in the eye after this?*

"People forget!" Pete Townshend screamed back.

He shut off the shower and stepped out into the steamy bathroom, drying himself off as quickly as he could. His left hip, the entire upper part of his thigh, ached, and he could see the suggestion of a nasty bruise beginning to well on his skin. Steve ran a hand along it. It had been years since he had a bruise like this; it reminded him of Brandee and the rough sex she had enjoyed. She played to win, and she played dirty sometimes, even giving him a black eye once by accident.

Steve rubbed his hair with the towel as he walked toward his bedroom. He stepped into a pair of boxers and slid a clean t-shirt over his head, then padded into the kitchen, his bare feet curling in response to the cold linoleum floor. His eyes drifted to the framed map, traced the red zigzags of travel his ex-wife had delineated for them. He grabbed a beer from the fridge and popped open the can, still looking at the map. Before he could stop himself, he picked up his cell phone and tapped the Favorites tab on his call screen. She was still there, at the top, a mischievous grin beaming from the thumbnail of her face. Steve ran his finger slowly over the photo, then brought the phone to his ear.

It rang four times before picking up. *Hey,* her voice intoned. *You've reached Brandee. Leave a message and I'll call you back.* It was the same message she'd used since buying the phone five years earlier. Steve quickly tapped the red END prompt and placed the phone, screen down, on the counter.

He took a long swig of beer.

Chastising himself, he picked up the phone again and tapped Brandee's contact.

Hey. You've reached Brandee. Leave a message and I'll call you back.

He tapped the red prompt, then tapped her thumbnail again.

Hey. You've reached B—

When he tapped the END prompt this time, he left his phone on the counter and walked away from it. He stopped at the sink, drank from the can, and gazed out the window. Snow fell heavily, already disguising his backyard under a shroud of white. The large pine tree at the corner of his yard drooped its branches slightly, the clusters of sharp green needles holding fast to their frozen veil.

Steve tipped his head backward and swallowed the rest of his beer in three gulps. He considered grabbing a second can from the fridge, then buried the suggestion. It was after midnight. The anxiety insistently poking at his gut was nothing more than aftershocks from his earlier escape out the window. He just needed some sleep.

Without bothering to turn off the lights, he abandoned the empty can on the edge of the sink, looked at the snow again, then walked slowly to his bedroom. He didn't bother to set an alarm.

* * *

Something was in Jackie Ketchum's room.

She awoke with a start and sat up in bed, her head screaming with a stabbing pain in return. She gripped the side of her face in response, willing her eyes to adjust to the darkness. Snippets of a quickly fading dream flashed across her memory. She had been standing in the middle of a large, open yard with a small shed in its corner. The door to the shed opened, and out walked Rose Bennett, the elderly woman who lived with her daughter two houses down. Only she didn't walk: she glided from between the doors of the structure, then drifted ethereally toward Jackie, her hands held out in front of her as if she were feeling her way through a pitch-black room.

Suddenly, Jackie was no longer in the yard but trapped in a tight enclosure, an empty closet of brick walls. She might have been in a chimney, but a chimney capped with a ceiling of red brick and no fireplace below. A brick coffin. She pressed her hand against the blocks beside her and watched her skin crinkle and melt before her eyes as if being cooked by a flame.

Jackie pressed her fingers against her temples. The darkness in the room did not abate, but Jackie could make out a fuzzy shape swaying near her dresser. Her mind took inventory of the contents of her nightstand, searching for a weapon. If she could reach down slowly, retrieve the bat from under her bed, she might stand a chance at whatever was standing there, waiting for her in her bedroom. Instead, Jackie leaned on her right side, felt the headache radiate around her cheekbones, and pressed the switch on the table lamp.

On the edge of her dresser sat Jimmy Changa, his fat fluffy tail twitching with interest at his owner's nocturnal activity. Jackie glanced at the digital clock. It was only a few minutes past twelve. "If you think I'm getting up now to feed you breakfast, you've got another thing coming," Jackie told the cat. In response, Jimmy leaped from his perch and landed on the thin strip of wood comprising the windowsill. He pushed insistently at the edge of the window shade with his large orange head until his body slipped awkwardly behind it, the protrusion of blinds letting in a sliver of street-lamp and starlight.

Jackie blinked her eyes. As the pain in her head simmered to a dull throb, she swung her legs outside of the blankets and climbed out of bed. She pulled gently on the bottom of the window shade and let it roll up to the top of the pane. Her side yard was covered in a thin blanket of snow and more of it poured from the sky, saturating the air with white flakes. Beyond that, the streetlamp cast long shadows across Steve's backyard, giving it the appearance of being streaked with something dark and nefarious, cast-offs of blood spray in a vicious attack.

Something moved. This time, it wasn't inside her house but outside, in the backyard, in Steve's backyard.

Jackie pressed her face to the glass. Sure enough, a hulking figure—much too thin to be Steve, but much too large to be Carol's wandering mother—leaned against one of the tall trees that straddled the property line. Suddenly, the strange shape darted from shadow to shadow in the dim illu-mination, its speed incongruous with its corporeality. Jimmy Changa spied it, too. He fixed his eyes on the interloper, a low growl emitting from his throat.

Below the feline drone of warning, however, Jackie swore she heard something else, a sound drifting from the outside. It resembled whispering, but a moaning whisper, like whoever, or whatever was making it ached with pain. She pressed her ear to the window, then pulled away quickly, the cold glass making her shiver. The whispering continued, though Jackie could not decipher its content. She closed her eyes, trying to focus on the sound. Each time a word came into focus, it evaporated as quickly as it arrived, an exercise in capturing snowflakes.

Jimmy Changa crouched awkwardly on the thin sill. His ears folded back along his head until they practically disappeared. Jackie watched her cat's eyes reflected in the dark glass. The pupils grew wide, and Jimmy, his attention rapt with the figure skulking about their neighbor's yard, opened his mouth and hissed.

* * *

Carol Bennett sat in the upholstered wingback chair in the corner of Rose's room. She opened the clock app on her phone and set an alarm for four hours later. The shades were open, and as the snow drifted lazily past the glass, the light from the streetlamps diffused through the flakes, casting the room with a dim, ethereal glow.

She would have to invest in a bed alarm, she realized. The doctor had advised her to do so after Rose's first nocturnal wandering, but Carol had been reluctant to take such an extreme measure, opting instead to prop a baby monitor atop Rose's nightstand. Even as she did this, Carol felt the shame of actively eavesdropping on her mother wash over her, but Rose seemed unfazed by it.

What is it you're afraid to hear? Rose signed. *It's not like you'll catch me talking to myself.* She laughed, then. Her own mother had laughed at the preventative measures Carol was taking to prevent Rose from harming herself.

The monitor had not worked. Carol slept through her mother's escape into the frigid evening and had only been awakened by the sound of Rose's banging on their ancient shed.

It's inside, and it wants to come out.

Carol felt a pang of nausea swirl in her stomach. Rose

had signed this, over and over, as Carol guided her mother gently back indoors, the well-meaning neighbor standing speechless at the gate, watching their every move.

Who are you talking about? Carol finally asked Rose once the woman was back under the covers. *Who is "it?"*

Rose only shrugged. Then, before she closed her eyes and drifted back to sleep, she signed one more thing. *I could hear it, crouched down, hiding in there.*

Who, Mom? Carol signed, but her mother did not open her eyes. A thin snore mumbled from between her lips, and Carol stood a long time, watching her, before retrieving a blanket from her own bed and settling into Rose's chair with it. She needed to get some sleep, at least an hour or two more, or Carol knew she would be a zombie in front of her students if they did, indeed, have school the next day. Just as she closed her eyes, the skin of her eyelids was alight, and as she opened them again, she discovered her mother staring at her, the lamp on the bedside table shining brightly.

"What is it?" Carol said out loud, then repeated the question with her hands. "Are you okay, Mom?"

Rose looked from the window back to her daughter. *Do you remember that poem by Robert Frost? The one about the snow, about the empty field of snow? The one you memorized in high school for that competition?*

Carol thought for a moment. *Desert Places,* she signed. *Yes. Why?*

Rose watched the flakes increase in velocity behind the glass, then turned back to her daughter. *It smothers them in their houses,* she signed. *But it can't scare me.*

I don't understand, signed Carol. *Who? Who are you talking about?*

Rose jutted her chin toward the window, then turned the rest of her face to follow it. The two women sat in silence, Carol studying her mother's serene expression as she watched the storm. Then, she rested her head against the crook of the seat's back and closed her eyes, finally drifting off to a dreamless sleep.

Rose, however, remained awake, never taking her eyes from the windowpane.

* * *

The table beneath her was uncomfortable, and Kim O'Dell tried to disguise a pained expression as her shoulder blades banged against the hardwood over and over.

She was in her own dining room, but somehow, the room existed in someone else's house, the threshold to the kitchen revealing a stranger's Day-Glo orange decor, the edge of a refrigerator painted a strange, sunlit yellow.

And who were these people surrounding them? Kim glanced nervously about as Tom pounded like a metronome on top of her naked body. Five or six wide-eyed strangers, also naked, sat in wooden chairs encircling them, studying their every move with fascination. Unaffected by the voyeurs, Tom grunted; a fat bead of hot sweat drizzled from his forehead and snaked into Kim's left eye, stinging and momentarily blinding her.

"Baby?" Kim asked meekly, gently patting her husband's back. "Babe?"

Tom ignored her. The sound of her bones slamming against the wood grew louder, the reverberation quivering down her spine like a tuning fork. The stranger nearest to her leaned closer and rested a fat hairy hand on her upper arm. Kim flinched and tried to curl her body away, but the weight of her husband rooted her firmly in place.

Tom bucked twice more, urgently, then froze in place, groaning in an octave Kim knew very well. It would be over soon, she thought. Tom would roll off of her and she could escape. Except, it wasn't over: not exactly. The sex concluded, but as Tom furled away from her body, Kim discovered she was no longer naked. Instead, she was wearing an avocado green smock, the same color as the reusable grocery bags she utilized each weekly trip to the market. Instead of panting strangers surrounding her at the table, Tom, fully dressed, along with Dylan and Aaron, sat in chairs at her sides and feet.

"What—" Kim began. She tried to sit up but found that she was bolted in place: literally pinned to the table with metal turkey lacers driven through the edges of her dress like diner spikes. She looked to her husband, then to her sons for help, but they only stared back at her blankly.

Suddenly, Tom grasped her ankles and pulled them together, holding them tightly in one hand. In the other, he brandished a carving knife, the kind he used each holiday to serve Kim's carefully prepared roasts. Kim's eyes darted about the table, looking for the food Tom was set to slice, then realized with horror that she was the only thing on the table.

Dylan and Aaron leaned closer to her, each holding a fork and steak knife. Thick streams of drool dripped from their mouths.

"What are you doing?!" Kim shouted, but Tom's face did not register that he heard her. He plunged the carving knife into the side of her foot and sawed back and forth. There was no pain, not even the sensation of a tickle, but Kim screamed. Tom made another incision, and another, and then, using the tip of the cutting instrument like a skewer, stabbed the wedge of Kim he'd excised from her foot, brought it to his mouth, and began to chew. As if this signaled the start of the meal, the boys on either side of her began to spear and slice at her upper arms, the side of her torso, the curve of her hip.

Everywhere she had ever pinched an inch, Kim thought, still screaming.

Until Tom appeared at her forehead and angled the tip of his knife at her eyeball.

She awoke suddenly, her nightgown and the top sheet below her drenched with sweat. Tom continued to doze unfettered beside her, a small snore snaking from his mouth and around the side of his pillow. Ever so slowly, Kim rolled the covers from her body and slid her body out. Although the room was not cold, a shiver ran across her back. The wetness of her clothes made her skin feel clammy and anemic, and she quickly peeled the sodden gown from her body and replaced it with one of Tom's t-shirts from the top of the hamper.

She unplugged her phone from the charging station on her vanity and tiptoed into the bathroom, taking great care not to wake up her screen until she had shut the door behind her and turned on the light. The internet had been a bone of contention. Tom had begged her to stop visiting medical websites; once, during an argument, he threatened to block them on her phone altogether. Kim didn't just consult them, he argued. She rode them like waterslides, disappearing into windowless bunkers from which she did not emerge, not without prescription intervention.

She would stay away from medical websites, Kim silently promised herself. She wouldn't even look at their summaries on the page of results. *Then why are you hiding in the bathroom?* Kim asked herself. She shook off the question and sat on the edge of the tub.

Outside, the snow had doubled in velocity, and Kim glanced at the empty street beyond her reflection before opening up a search engine and carefully typing *nightmare about being eaten meaning*. A series of Quora forums as well as a few dream dictionary sites popped up in the response, but Kim tapped a Reddit link, opening her app to the subreddit r/Dreams. Someone had begun a thread two years earlier, but the most recent response appeared to have been added only a few months previous.

I had a dream about being eaten alive by my family, the entry read. *What does that mean?*

More than a dozen site members jumped into the discussion to offer their expertise.

It's a reflection of your self-doubt, your feelings of being overwhelmed and overworked. Life is literally eating you alive. Is your family demanding too much of you these days?

Your [sic] being devoured by responsibility.

You think your family is parasitizing you. You know, like eating you up while giving you nothing in return.

It's more about you than about your family. You are the one who is being false, and you feel guilty, and that guilt is eating you up inside.

A fear of losing control is consuming you.

Definitely something is consuming you. Your marriage, your kids, your household. Get a maid and a nanny.

OMG I had a dream that I was eating my family. So freaky. Right?

Kim closed the window on the search engine. She did not feel consumed by her family. She loved them, loved being a mother and a wife.

Didn't she?

What will you do when the boys go off to college, get married, start families of their own somewhere far away? a stranger's voice asked from inside her head. She would still be a wife, she told the stranger. *Only if you keep your husband happy.* She thought of the proposal Tom had made, the one about attending the sex club, and the image of him cutting off the bottom of her foot flashed across her memory.

Another voice, one Kim equated with her own, only ten or twenty years in the future, chided her softly. *You made that bed,* it said.

She stood up and walked to the window, shaded her eyes

from the glare with her hand against the glass, and looked outside. Everything was still. Even the gray squirrels that flitted about the lawns had hunkered down in some unseen grotto to ride out the storm.

Kim put her hand down and turned off the light. She plugged her phone back into the charger and climbed into bed beside her husband.

Excerpt from the documentary:

Sticky Fingers:
Unsolved Mysteries of the
Tar Heel State

Narrated by Peter Thomas
Vestron Pictures, 1989

February, 1973. Residents remained frozen in the plummeting temperatures as well as in fear following the wave of cold, ice, and snow blanketing the coast of North Carolina. Beachfront communities such as Wilmington received more than fifteen inches of accumulation. High winds created snowdrifts nearly twice that height, halting travel along Interstates 40 and 140 and isolating residents in their homes for the weekend.

When Bruce Livvy did not show up for work at the Market Street Buick dealership Monday morning, the office manager sent another employee to check on his welfare, as a number of telephone lines had been damaged by gale-force winds and heavy ice. To the employee's horror, Livvy, along with his wife and college-aged son, were discovered murdered, their bodies piled neatly in the family's bathtub. Velma Livvy had been strangled while the cause of death for both her husband and son was drowning, even though the tub where the three were discovered was bone dry.

Tire track analysis aided authorities in tracking down the assailants. Police arrested three men in connection with the killings. David Wayne claimed to have only served as the getaway driver but stated that the family was killed as part of a hit sanctioned by the Dixie Mafia, an organized crime group that has operated out of Georgia since the 1960s.

Sadly, however, the Livvys were unfortunate collateral damage. While driving from Senoia to Wilmington on Saturday, the men were caught in a snow squall. Whiteout conditions made travel impossible for many hours. When the heart of the storm had passed, Wayne claims to have remained disorientated, directing the vehicle to not only the wrong home but to the wrong location altogether. The intended targets lived in Wilmington, Delaware.

Delaware received just over a foot of snow accumulation in the storm.

Weathermen are blaming El Niño for the above-average snowfall pummeling the Southeastern seaboard this season, pointing out the inches that have amassed from Maryland to northern Florida since the Christmas holiday. The region typically receives only one to two inches of snow accumulation each year.

Wayne, along with his accomplices, are being held without bail pending arraignment. Wayne continues to insist that he has no memory of the murder and can only account for the hours leading up to and following the family's demise.

Chapter Seven

Several inches of snow had accumulated by the time John Stephenson stood in the unadorned picture window, watching the neighborhood sleep. A solid sugary crust was sprinkled atop the thirsty blacktop and dead January grass, and the previous day's news had warned that more than a foot would follow. John scratched his cheek, the two-day-old scruff there echoing with sandpaper in response.

A city plow trundled up the road, anxious to get to another part of the city. The tire tracks left in its wake were the only blemish along the expanse of white. Even the birds and nocturnal creatures that roamed nightly, investigating garbage cans and nest-friendly flotsam, were nowhere to be seen.

John's neighbors across the street, Dan and Janet, kept a predictable schedule: so much so that when he caught a few winks of sleep during the day, he could gaze out at their house upon awakening and know from the placement of their cars, the illumination in their windows, or the appearance of one of them walking the dog what hour it was. He knew that Janet stayed an hour later at work on Tuesdays and that Dan climbed onto their elliptical machine every Monday, Wednesday, and Friday morning while watching *The Price is Right.*

And, twice a week since December, Steve, his neighbor who lived two houses over, traipsed over to sleep with Janet on the sly. The guest room of Dan and Janet's craftsman bungalow was in the front corner of the house, and Janet often neglected to pull the shades.

The digital clock on John's cable television receiver was the only source of light in John's living room, casting a sleepy red glow along his hardwood floor and furniture. It was two hours past midnight, but John stood wide awake, the insistent cold pressing against the windowpane, urging him to wrap his arms around himself for warmth. Only a few hours before, John watched Dan's truck pull into the couple's driveway incongruously hours earlier than expected: John at first assumed his own clocks were incorrect. Seconds later, like a scene from a 1970s sitcom, Steve slipped from their front side window and into Janet's dormant flower beds and raced discombobulated across the street, his open flannel shirt blowing behind him like a plaid cape, only to be abruptly grazed by their neighbor Jackie's car. John damn near expected a leisure-suited Don Knotts to come running up the street after all of them.

As the lights in their house blinked on in slow sequence to signal Dan's progression through the house, a wet-haired Janet wriggled into her clothes and appeared on the couple's driveway, a leashed Noodle in tow. The snow began, first as a few errant wisps of white, then in great gusts like someone had taken a knife to a pillowy cloud, sending a deluge of fat feathery flakes sailing to the earth. By the time Janet was halfway up the block, the pair was leaving visible tracks on the sidewalk behind them. John did notice something strange, a quirky bit of behavior that he paid little mind— Lord knew, he'd seen just about everything in his daily observations of the street's residents: Janet stopped abruptly, crouched down to the ground, and pressed her face against it. She stayed posed this way for nearly five minutes, moving only to shoo the dog's investigative snout from her face. When she rose to her feet again at last, she did not continue up the street but turned and walked directly back to her house, the confused canine making a quick pit stop on the tree belt before slackening the leash.

John watched Noodle lumber faithfully behind his owner until the dog disappeared inside the house. John's heart ached a bit when he saw the neighborhood pets. Since Louis left, John had lived alone, and he had not stepped even a toe outside of his three-season porch since the 2020 pandemic. John had always battled a seesaw of depression and anxiety, but he didn't know why the global incident had been the final straw. He wasn't particularly afraid of germs: hell, he'd skipped his annual flu shot and despite Louis' look of disgust, regularly gorged himself on the samples offered at the local warehouse shopping conglomerate each time they visited. Somehow, however, the idea of a virus, an entity skulking about the outside world just waiting for an opportunity to strike, consumed him.

Louis had been patient at first, and the two of them managed to stave off the mounting claustrophobia affecting most of the world. Everyone had been trapped inside their homes for most of the year, after all, but John and Louis had a bumper crop of technology at their fingertips. Louis was a system analyst for a major telecommunication company, and when the world came to a virtual standstill, his position launched into overdrive. Overnight, their house transformed into a hub of modems, wires, and screens.

John watched the sky silently spread layer after layer of delicate white icing over the staid neighborhood. Dan was always good about shoveling John's walk for him, even though he refused to take any payment in return. He suspected this was, in part, because Dan felt sorry for John, or perhaps he saw it as some sort of payback, as Louis had often raked their neighbors' lawns or run the snow blower along their sidewalks each time he set aside time to clear his own. Louis was thoughtful that way.

* * *

On the day he informed John of his leaving, he had made certain the pathway to the door was completely clear of ice, spending an extra hour meticulously scraping every bit of slipperiness and drowning the pavement with melting crystals until the ground was dry as bone. Then, he marched back into the house, removed his heavy coat and hat, poured himself a fresh cup of coffee, and told John the news.

"I'll get help," John pleaded in response. "I will this time. I promise."

Louis peeled his hands from around the ceramic mug of coffee and placed them on top of John's. They were hot as fire. "I'm sorry. It's too late." He looked down at the table. "I should have said something months ago."

"But—" John began, but he did not finish the sentence as there was nothing to complete it. The two were silent for a long moment, the faint ticking of the wall clock painfully loud. "Where are you going?" John said finally.

Louis sighed. "Missy has an extra bedroom. I'm moving in with her and Erik for the time being. Then, Donna said there might be a house going up for sale down the street from her. I don't know. I guess I'll see." He removed his hands from John's and rested them casually on his lap.

John looked up at the ceiling, blinking back tears. "Missy and Erik know? Donna knows? Who else did you discuss breaking up with me with?" He sniffed. "Everyone knows that you're miserable. Everyone but me." He looked at

Louis. "What is wrong with me that I didn't see it?" He reached out to touch Louis' arm, but Louis jerked away.

"Look," Louis said, his tone suddenly business-like. "I made arrangements to have my mail forwarded to Missy's, and I contacted the cable company: you can call them tomorrow and transfer the account into your name." He reached for the coffee cup, raised it halfway to his lips, then set it back on the table. "I'll text you here and there, but I asked Dan to check in with you, just to make sure you're okay." He leaned forward and pulled his phone from his back pocket, tapped the screen, then showed it to John. "There are a few grocery delivery services in the area. I checked them out. And—" He turned the screen back to himself, tapped it a few more times, and returned it to John's view. "Here are some therapists that work remotely. You can't live like this for the rest of your life, John." He dropped the screen and placed the phone gently, facedown, on the table next to the cup. "You just can't."

John swallowed hard but said nothing. There was no talking Louis out of this; he understood that, but it didn't make the news easier to digest.

When he packed his Ford Focus with suitcases and badly taped cardboard boxes the next day, Louis left more than John's share of the electronic devices, unable to abandon his partner completely to a life of self-imposed isolation. He also left his cat, a fat orange tabby named Jonesy who refused to wear a collar. One morning, when John steeled himself enough to reach an arm onto the concrete steps where the delivery person had mistakenly left his grocery order, Jonesy seized the opportunity to make for the hills. Too paralyzed with fear to pursue him, John watched helplessly as the only other three-dimensional life form in his life escaped to the next yard, never to return. Months later, when he saw Jonesy's round face poking out from behind the blinds of his neighbor Jackie's window, he felt a tug of jealousy, but at least he knew the animal was safe, not trapped in a cage at the local shelter or as the dinner of a savvy predator.

Louis, for his part, stopped checking in on John and his cat after only three months. After that, their relationship was well past the safe-to-sell-by date, the expiration having come and gone, and Louis was free to toss any connection to John in the compost pile, leaving his former boyfriend plenty of rope to wallow in his cemented agoraphobia and eventual voyeurism forever.

John owned his house outright and had invested wisely before the world came to a temporary standstill. He could remain in his house unfettered, content to receive his necessities by mail, and adapted, albeit in a maladjusted manner, to a life of virtually zero human interaction. He slept when he was tired, clicked about television channels when he was bored, and watched the neighborhood as it ebbed and flowed.

* * *

Despite being unable to sleep, John was tired. There was no getting around that. John was always tired these days, even as his mind stubbornly refused to lie still for more than an hour at a time. When the exhaustion got to be too much, like it had been that evening, John acquiesced to his online doctor's suggestion that he take the medication he'd been prescribed, the only one of the slew of drugs in the succession of trial and error to knock him out, not just for an hour or two but for a solid six to eight. The trouble was, the drug worked too well, and John's everyday anxiety was overshadowed by the suggestion that perhaps he would become addicted to the substance, and what would happen if another global standstill occurred and he was unable to secure his prescription? It was better that he limit use to once a week, maximum. On the other nights, he wandered his empty house like a ghost and lived vicariously through the middle-aged brethren who surrounded him in the snug houses within sight of his windows.

The narcotic took at least a half hour to root itself securely in his system, and watching the snow cover the dormant neighborhood would pass the time until it did. Except, the street wasn't fully asleep. Not all of it.

Across from him, the unadorned windows of Janet and Dan's guest room filled with light. Janet stood at the far end of the room, her hand resting on the wall switch. She paused, then moved closer to the window. Even after months of watching her roll about the bed with Steve, John was shocked to see her standing stark naked. She reached the window, and keeping her arms hidden behind her back, pressed her body against it, her bare breasts spreading like batter against the hard, cold glass.

John hesitantly stepped backward but kept his eyes fixed on his neighbor. Of course she would be interested in watching the storm: in the beam of the streetlamps, the incessant streaming of fat white flakes was serenely picturesque, almost hypnotic. However, Janet wasn't looking at the snow.

She was staring, very intently, at John, a crooked smile oozing from one side of her mouth.

After a long minute, Dan appeared in the doorway behind Janet. John watched him call out to her, the soundtrack muted like an old-timey picture show. Janet did not respond, but continued to stare, unblinking, across the street at her neighbor's dark picture window. With a look of exhausted frustration plastered across his face, Dan walked quickly to his partner. Even as he approached her in the starkly lit room, Janet did not acknowledge his presence, not until he was immediately behind her.

Then, she pulled her arms back in front of her body.

John saw the knife, the large Santoku carving knife, but his mind could not make sense of what Janet was doing. Before Dan could react to her, Janet turned and plunged the blade deep into Dan's chest. His face twisted in confusion, then leaped immediately to horror as Janet pulled out the blade and stabbed him again. And again. And again. Janet's stabbing grew progressively faster and more primal as she thrust the weapon over and over into her partner's lungs and heart, each movement adding to the crimson red canvas opening on his torso until Dan's knees folded beneath him and he collapsed downward and out of sight.

Janet did not follow him but stood motionless, her back to the window and her eyes fixed on the floor. John reflexively brought his hand to his mouth, stifling a scream. Surely, this was a dream. He knew that drug was a problem. He must have dozed off and not realized it.

When she turned back to the window, Janet's chest was covered in blood. John moved closer to his own window, praying Janet would see him. She must be sleepwalking, John thought. She is sleepwalking and needs to wake up. "Wake up!" John called. His voice sounded strange in the silent house. "Janet, wake up!" He over-enunciated each syllable, willing his neighbor to see him and understand his plea.

Janet was not listening to anyone: anyone John could see, anyway. Her mouth widened once more in an unsettling grin, but her eyes stared blankly forward, no longer looking at John but at something in the unseen distance. She brought the blade of the knife to her own throat, its silver edge sticky with blood and pulp. Her eyes flittered quickly to John's, and in one quick swoop, Janet drove the knife into her own throat and jerked it sideways, the jagged wound immediately vomiting bright red. Then, she crumpled into a heap out of John's field of vision.

John screamed. He raised his hands to the picture

window and banged his palms rhythmically against the glass. Each movement of his arms felt heavier than the previous, as if he were swimming in quicksand. John stopped moving his hands and held them down at his sides. He looked downward and took a deep breath. The world around him shifted, then spun slightly. He felt dizzy and weak, so he allowed himself to sink downward. The hardwood floor felt nearly as cool as the glass. He pressed his cheek against it, the feverish heat on his face drinking in the temporary relief.

He would call the police, John told himself. He would call the police and report what he saw, and maybe, no: surely, an officer would come to his door and assure him that no, he had just been dreaming. His neighbors were perfectly fine, and would he be interested in getting some help for his dreadful nervous condition? The officer knew of just the treatment center. One call, and the transport would be on their way. John, of course, would need to be asleep during the transition. The very idea of stepping outside made his breathing catch in his throat. If John would just lie down on the couch, just for a moment, the officer would make him a nice cup of herbal tea, and the medics would be arriving soon, stocked with the most potent sedatives on the planet.

John considered this as he climbed cautiously onto his sofa, his mind willing itself to cover up with a thick wool blanket the image of Janet standing with the blade at her neck. *Nothing to see here, go about your day*, John thought sleepily. Then, he let himself fall sideways, his head resting cozily on a throw pillow, his eyelids feeling heavier by the second. He would surrender to the narcotic, and when he awoke, all would make sense again.

John assured himself of this, then he closed his eyes and felt himself fall backward, away from his house and his street and his bloody neighbors, his dead neighbors, and sink deep into the dark water of dreamless sleep.

Chapter Eight

"Okay," Brandee said, standing with one hand placed awkwardly on her hip and the other gesturing toward the map like a game show model. "Here's where we gotta knuckle down."

Steve folded his arms in front of his chest and leaned back in the kitchen chair. "I'm ready," he responded, mock-serious.

Brandee smiled broadly at him. *Jesus, she is cute,* Steve thought. Even in her early thirties, Brandee could be as bouncy as a college freshman when she wanted to be. He liked that about her. The two of them were never stuffy, even when solemnity was required. At the break between viewings at his mother's wake, she had dragged him behind the funeral home and handed him a one-hitter filled with some of the most potent weed he'd smelled in his life. "You need this," she said, and then produced a plastic lighter from the inside pocket of her blazer. The two of them smoked up, and smack in the middle of the second viewing, it caught up with him. A regular from Whistler's appeared in the condolence line, and for the life of him, he couldn't recall what drink she always ordered. She had been coming to the bar for years—hell, even before Steve was bartending, maybe even before he had been legal enough to drink—and he could. not. remember.

He elbowed Brandee. "What does that woman order when she comes in?" he whispered into her ear.

Brandee slowly turned back to him, keeping her face a blank slate. She said nothing, only stared, her eyes verdant pools rippling in the wind.

"What does she order?" Steve repeated, the sound of his own voice echoing off the inside of his brain like screams inside a natatorium. The woman was only a few visitors away, and Steve felt anxiety rise in his torso.

Brandee pressed her mouth close to his ear. "You want to know what your regular orders for a drink?" she whispered. "At your mother's funeral?"

Steve felt his mind hopscotch two spaces backward. He was too high. He shouldn't have smoked as much as he did. He should have eaten something at lunch. Should've, could've, would've. It was too late for regrets. No take backsies. "Yes," he answered, his face still turned forward. A bead of sweat drizzled slowly from his forehead to his jaw.

The regular stood in front of him. She hugged him suddenly, though the entanglement more resembled a tortilla encircling its filling than anything else; Steve stood, stick straight, his arms at his sides, as she wrapped her arms around his shoulders and stayed that way for a beat or two too long.

Brandee, for her part, reached into her inner jacket pocket and produced a tiny bottle of Jameson. "Thank you for coming," she said, clutching the regular's nearest hand in hers and transferring the whiskey nip into it. She flashed a somber countenance at the woman, who looked down at the newly acquired item in her hand and released her grip on Steve immediately. A tiny grin peeked from the corner of her mouth, and she walked away without saying anything more.

Brandee continued to face forward, her expression blank, but she elbowed Steve and contorted her lips so that she resembled a cartoon character speaking out of one side of its mouth. "I got you," she whispered, and Steve reached up and squeezed her forearm in return.

As she stood, gesturing toward their map on the kitchen wall, she produced a fat magic marker from the back pocket of her jeans. "Okay," she continued. "Here's the plan, Stan. Every time we travel to a place, we trace the route going from us—" She paused to hold her marker on a small dot on the left side of Massachusetts. "To our destination." She squinted at the map, then slowly dragged the tip of the pen along Route 91 down to the bottom of Connecticut, then hesitated before changing to Route 95 and following it south.

Steve leaned back in his chair, watching. "But we didn't drive. We flew."

Brandee reached Savannah and pulled the marker from the page. Still holding it uncapped, the bright red tip pointing to the ceiling, she stepped back to examine her work. "I know, but the whole straight-line thing, even if it's not done with string, gives off too much of an FBI serial killer vision board vibe." She turned to look at Steve. "What do you think?" She smiled again, the toothy one that still gave Steve a rush of warmth in his stomach.

He smiled back. "I think you should do San Antonio next."

* * *

The memory of this still caused a visceral reflex in Steve nearly seven years later as he sat in the same chair, staring at the map on the wall. So many crooked crimson lines bleeding from the top right corner. He wondered, briefly, if Brandee ever thought about him, about their travel adventures. She must have seen the missed calls from the previous night, yet she hadn't responded. Would she call him back, he wondered? Text him? Or had she closed their chapter completely, shut the book tight and tossed it into the fire?

A gust of wind beat against his window, rattling the pane. Snow pounded the glass in angry fistfuls. Inside, safe from the weather and still wearing the tee and boxer shorts from the previous night, Steve tussled with a white powder of his own. He dumped a small pile of cocaine from the week's haul onto his kitchen table, chopped and scraped it briefly with the razor blade he kept in the kitchen's junk drawer, then bent over, covering one nostril as he inhaled it into the back of his throat.

He wasn't due at Whistler's until the evening, and the news report predicted the storm to continue well past five o'clock. He half-jogged into his living room, switched on his turntable, and fingered the assemblage of LPs in the repurposed milk crate on the floor below it. He pulled out a record, pausing to stare at the cover, the members of The Who posing awkwardly around a tall concrete slab, then gingerly slipped the disc from its case. A moment after he placed the needle on the opening groove, a melodious echoing of Lowrey organ on a Marimba Repeat filled the room.

I could never live in an apartment building, Steve mused, the amphetamine effervescence bubbling up through his chest, tickling his brain. "My neighbors would break a broom, hitting the ceiling," he said, finishing the thought out loud, his voice oddly tinny under the swell of the music. He nudged the volume dial even higher, then skipped back into the kitchen.

As he snorted another white line, his cell phone rang. "Fuck!" Steve exclaimed. He had wanted Brandee to call back. He had wanted that very badly. But he didn't want to talk to her now, not while he was sailing somewhere near the ceiling, a barrage of thoughts shooting wildly about the room like a game of 52 Pick Up. He hopped quickly toward the counter and looked at the screen before tapping the CALL button.

"Yeah?" he said, the word drifting from his mouth and into his nostrils, swelling them with warmth. He used his free hand to squeeze his nose, then sniffed. "Yeah," he repeated, calmer, "this is Steve."

"Steve?" The voice was small, almost child-like, but Steve recognized it at once. "This is Kelly. I had your number in my phone from the Christmas party."

Steve's foot began to tap, much too fast to be keeping time with "Baba O'Riley." "Yeah, yeah," Steve said, sniffing again. "What's up?" *Oh shit*, he thought. Something happened. The bar burned down. She forgot to lock the door when she closed the night before; someone broke in and cleaned the place out. A pipe had burst in the cold. The lines for the kegs had rotted out. Aliens invaded and drank all of the liquor. His mind flipped through a succession of cue cards dictating every scenario.

"It's snowing pretty bad here," Kelly said. "Like, bad."

It's snowing here, too, Steve thought. Where did she think he lived? Florida? "Yeah, yeah," he agreed, impatient. "It sure is."

"I...I don't think my Volkswagen is going to make it in the snow," she continued. "And I'm supposed to open today."

Steve glanced outside. The space beyond the pane was more white than air. He eyed the digital numbers on the microwave. Eleven-thirty. "Shouldn't you already be there?" he asked. The day shift ran eleven to five, sometimes six.

He heard her exhale from the other end of the line. "Uh, yeah," she stammered. "I thought—I thought I would be able to make it, but I can't even get out of my driveway. Besides, no one is going out in this mess right now."

Steve's thoughts raced. "I can get there for one," he said finally. "Let me just see if the storm lets up a bit. Then I can at least make a dent in the shoveling before I go." *And mellow out this high a bit*, he added silently.

"They're all wasted!" Roger Daltrey yelled ecstatically from the other room.

As if in concert with him, Kelly's volume immediately increased. "Oh, thank you, thank you, thank you!" she shouted. "I owe you one, Steve."

"Yeah, yeah," he said reluctantly. "Stay warm," he added, but she had hung up without saying goodbye. He looked out the kitchen window again. Anything he shoveled now would be replaced by mid-afternoon, easy, but at least there would be less to move when he returned home after midnight, he reasoned. Besides, it was becoming much too warm in the house. He needed some fresh air.

Steve got dressed, then bundled himself up tight in a heavy coat, scarf, and wool hat. Brandee had given him that hat when they were dating. They had traveled to New York City to see the Christmas tree at Rockefeller Center but had a fight an hour before arriving. Steve couldn't remember what the argument had been about, no matter how hard he tried, but he did recall that Brandee refused to take a photo with him in front of the tree. Her nose had been rubbed red from crying, and she didn't want him to remember her that way, she'd told him. And yet, that's all Steve could envision: Brandee, her makeup smudged and her skin even paler than usual, all of the sun and blood seeming to have drained from her body.

He tapped the garage door button on the wall of the kitchen, then steeled himself for the rush of cold as he opened the door. Sure enough, a gust of crystallized wind pelted his face as he walked onto the driveway. It felt good. Refreshing.

He snatched the shovel from its peg on the garage wall and pushed it along the perimeter of his front lawn and down to the sidewalk. The snow was high—at least six or seven inches had accumulated—but it was relatively light, and Steve cursed himself for having forgotten to wear his earbuds. He seemed to clear the front walk in no time and hummed the refrain of "Going Mobile" as he continued onto Jackie's sidewalk and shoveled that as well, though the bare pavement was already dusted with more snow by the time he circled back to his house. He contemplated moving on to John, the neighborhood recluse, and clearing his walk as well, but then he remembered: Dan and Janet were immediately across the street. What if Dan came out of the house? Wanted to confront him?

You can't hide from him forever, a voice inside of Steve's head admonished. Then, it sidled into a soft shoe and added mournfully, *No one knows what it's like to be the bad man.*

Are you quoting "Behind Blue Eyes?" a second Steve voice inquired.

Why, you are correct, sir, the first Steve voice responded happily. An acoustic guitar melody piped in from somewhere unseen behind them, strumming the rest of the song's opening.

Steve replaced the shovel on its hook, removed his hat, and wiped his face with it. Even under the partial sanctuary of the garage's roof, his newly exposed ears flushed red against the wind chill. A sudden gust vomited a spray of snow onto the cement floor, and that is when Steve heard it. A tinkling, like an electronic xylophone, echoed from the street. Something about it sounded so familiar, a pop-like reimagining of Mike Oldfield's "Tubular Bells," only sped up and squeezed through a synthesizer.

He stepped back out onto his driveway and continued

slowly, trying to determine its source. No one was outside, and the few tire tracks woven along the road had long since been covered in multiple inches of white. He clutched his hat harder in his hand. The faraway music continued but its volume did not change, no matter how far he ventured toward the curb. Instead, a faint whispering joined it, not as a separate sound but as a spoken word monologue to accompany it.

A performance piece, Steve thought, then stopped to wipe his face again, the snow that had stuck to the wool melting instantly to wet against his skin. *The coke*, he realized. It was still ricocheting around his brain. He had picked up an ear worm of "Eminence Front" without realizing it and it was wriggling to the surface of his unconscious.

An image of Brandee, elbowing him a few feet away from his mother's corpse resting in its satin casket, flashed across his memory. *I got you.* Steve shook his head and wrenched the hat back onto his head before walking quickly back to the door.

The temperature inside the house was sweltering. When had he jacked up the heat? Steve peeled the wet over-clothes from his body and draped them over the kitchen chairs to dry, but he was still sweating profusely ten minutes later and unbuttoned his flannel shirt, took it off, and pushed his jeans to the floor. He stepped gingerly out of them and padded into the living room to check the reading on the thermostat.

He had left the record player on repeat. The needle's arm caressed the first piano bars of the final track of side one, "The Song is Over," but Steve ignored it, walking immediately to the digital readout on the wall monitor. Sixty-eight. That was higher than he usually kept it, but it wasn't tropical. Had he turned on the oven without remembering? He admonished himself for being so irresponsible. When had he become this person, he asked himself as he walked back to the kitchen. When had he become a man who did a bump before noon, alone in his home? When had he become a man who, in a world of available women, chose to sleep with his buddy's girlfriend?

When had Janet let herself into his house?

He stopped dead, his feet, clad only in socks, sliding slightly on the smooth flooring with his abruptness. Sure enough, Janet stood in his kitchen, bundled in her winter coat and hat, a fresh coating of snow quickly melting to teardrops along her shoulders and head.

"Hey, you," Janet said. "I didn't mean to scare you. Your door was unlocked."

Steve stood silent for a long minute, still recovering from the shock. "I didn't hear you come in," he said. "Ever consider changing your profession to cat burglar?"

Janet smiled. "I'm getting too long in the tooth to scale down fire escapes," she retorted. "But hey, they say you're never too old to learn a new skill." She unzipped her jacket and shook it off, a smattering of water droplets dotting the floor like a Pollock painting. When she removed her hat, her hair stood up in sticky angles, and she self-consciously smoothed it with one hand. "I saw you shoveling," she continued, "and thought I'd come by and say hi, but you were already inside."

Steve shifted his weight from one foot to another. His socks had wet spots on them, so he awkwardly kicked them off. "I got called into work," he said. "I'm not sure why we're even opening. I'll be staring at the televisions alone all day. Well, until the plow guys finish their shifts and stop by."

The two said nothing for a long minute, and the house was completely silent as the needle reached the end of the record, pausing before returning itself to the first track.

Janet sighed and crossed her arms in front of her chest. She turned slightly and focused her attention on the map on the wall. "I remember when I first saw this," she said. A devious smile spread across the bottom of her face, but her eyes did not move. "It was that day I brought the Thanksgiving leftovers over. You remember?" She paused, then turned to look at Steve, the smile frozen in place.

Of course Steve remembered. Snapshot memories of the encounter clicked across his brain. Janet unwrapping the scarf. Janet unbuttoning her overcoat. Janet running her hand slowly down his chest. An insistent throbbing began to swell in his groin. "Yes," he replied finally, swallowing hard. "It's a good thing you brought that food. Another hour and we would have eaten each other."

She winked at him, then slowly walked closer. "You left so suddenly last night," she purred. "We never got a chance to say goodbye." Janet dipped her chin downward and looked up at him from under a sweep of hair that had fallen across her face. "I missed you."

Steve resisted the urge to reach out and touch her. "Jan —" he began. She lifted her arm and rested a hand on his shoulder. It was still cold from her traveling outside. Ice cold, actually. Even through the cotton fabric of his t-shirt, its frigidity sent a wave of shivers down his spine. "Didn't Dan wonder why you were showering in the guest bathroom," he asked, "why the bed was unmade?"

Janet cupped the edge of his shoulder in her icy palm. "No," she said. "He didn't say anything. They had double staffed the shift by mistake. Computer error. So, he volunteered to come home." She slid her hand slowly down his upper arm, the edge of her pinky resting on the exposed skin of his elbow. As graceful as a dancer, Janet leaned forward so that her mouth hovered just outside of his ear. She whispered something, something Steve did not understand but sounded vaguely familiar. *Like snow*, he thought, slightly confused. Her words sounded like the snow whistling outside.

Steve backed away an inch and gave a half-hearted

shrug. "I want you to stay, Janet," he admitted. "But...Jesus. We dodged a bullet last night. Don't you think we should cut our losses and walk away clean...while we still can?" He heard himself say the words, but a part of him felt like a phony. He didn't want Janet to leave, and he didn't want to stop seeing her. And yet, something nudged at him from the back of his brain, something—

Janet reached her other arm out and grasped his wrist, then slowly rotated his arm so that the underside of his forearm was exposed. She rested her forefinger in the crook of his elbow, then gently traced a line along his skin to his wrist. When Steve said nothing, she shifted her hand in an adagio to his other arm and did the same. Slowly, gently, the pad of her finger barely caressed him. Steve felt something shift inside him, the primal desire shove his rationality and guilt aside, into a dark, dust-bunnied corner where he didn't have to look at it, where he could ignore it, at least for a short while.

Still holding his arm in her hand, Janet dropped to her knees. She rested her cheek against the front of Steve's shorts, then moved one hand to the top of his thigh. She drew her hand downward, the tip of her middle finger raking along the hairs on his leg until it reached the edge of his knee. She looked up at Steve. "You don't have to be lonely, you know," she said. "We can keep having adventures, and no one has to know. No one but us."

Steve placed his hand on the back of her head and hugged her to him. "Oh, Jan..." he began. Her hair and cheeks were as cold as her hands, but he pulled her tighter, his erection pushing earnestly against her face. Steve closed his eyes, and a wave of vertigo washed over him. His spine felt suddenly unsteady, the muscles in his legs melting into jelly. He opened his eyes and shot out a hand to grasp onto the nearby chair to secure himself, but his hand felt sticky, wet.

Janet was no longer kneeling before him. She was nowhere in the room. He reached his hand back toward his face to examine it. It was covered in a dark red substance: something metallic smelling, viscous and gummy. Blood. His hands were covered in blood.

Steve looked down at himself in horror. His arms and upper legs were also covered in blood. Something shiny glinted from the floor beside his foot. It was the razor blade, the one he'd used to cut the cocaine. As he watched, fat drops of blood dotted it. They dripped from his right arm.

Steve looked at his arm, at where Janet had traced her finger. An ugly red trench had been opened from his elbow to his wrist, and bright red blood poured from it, saturating his shorts and legs. A matching channel was drawn on his other arm and on one of his thighs. On the remaining appendage was a dark red divot, a shallow well of blood erupting from its depths.

From the living room, Roger Daltrey insisted that he did not need to be forgiven.

Back in the kitchen, Steve Kline collapsed onto the hard linoleum floor. He stared upward at the map on the wall until it blurred and faded into black.

Excerpt from:

Press Conference,
Hampden County Sheriff's Office

Aired Friday, January —, 20— 16:00 ET
Please Note: This transcript is not edited and
may contain errors.

SHERIFF'S OFFICE SPOKESPERSON: Thank you all for coming today.

So far, eight bodies have been recovered in the neighborhood of [STREET NAME REDACTED] and [STREET NAME REDACTED] during routine clean-up following Winter Storm Mia. The area received more than twenty inches in snow accumulation from late Monday evening through Thursday morning. Joining us today is Police Superintendent Rawle Brummell and Dr. Elle Collins of the CDC, who will address questions regarding this matter. Right now, I will turn over today's conference to Superintendent Brummell. Thank you, sir. You may begin.

SUPERINTENDENT RAWLE BRUMMELL: Good afternoon, folks. I will provide some opening remarks followed by Dr. Collins, who will give an overview of what we know so far regarding this tragedy. I want to make very clear: there is no cause for alarm. Dr. Collins has been consulted only as a precaution as we investigate the cause of these deaths, and we intend to quash any innuendo or rumors that might be proliferating. There is no reason to be concerned, and I hope this update can put the public's mind at ease. After remarks, Dr. Collins and I will be happy to take your questions.

At approximately four p.m. on Wednesday, a body was discovered in the front seat of a vehicle in an apparent car accident that appears to have been caused, at least in part, by slippery road conditions. As the deceased did not have a cell phone on their person, representatives from the Sheriff's Office traveled to the deceased's home to notify next of kin. On their way to the home, a second body was discovered a snow bank a block away. Subsequent inquiries in the immediate vicinity of the first victim's home discovered more bodies. So far, the bodies of eight individuals living within a two-block radius have been discovered, and—

SHERIFF'S OFFICE SPOKESPERSON: [off camera] Nine, sir.

SUPERINTENDENT RAWLE BRUMMELL:
As I was saying, the bodies of EIGHT individuals living within a two-block radius have been discovered, and representatives from police and emergency services have been going house to house to check on the welfare of others in the area.

Cause of death is not consistent from victim to victim, and there appears to be no connection between the deaths except in one specific case. However, after a consultation with the Department of Public Health, we reached out to the Center for Disease Control for their assessment, given the proximity and unusual nature of the cases, and Dr. Collins has kindly agreed to participate in this news briefing to address any questions regarding health and safety.

DR. ELLE COLLINS:

Thank you, Superintendent Brummell. In my capacity as a representative of the CDC, I spoke with the coroner's office and reviewed the medical information surrounding each death, and I can state with relative certainty that this cluster of sudden deaths is not related to a viral epidemic. Initial serum testing, including immunoglobulin tests, did not indicate any elevation in immune response, including increased antibodies or any changes to white cell, lymphocyte, and/or eosinophil counts.

SUPERINTENDENT RAWLE BRUMMELL:

I will open the floor to questions. However, I want to remind everyone, we are only in the initial stages of this investigation. Please formulate your questions accordingly. I recognize there are a lot of questions, and we will try to answer as many of them as we can.

SHERIFF'S OFFICE SPOKESPERSON:

Thank you. The first question comes from Zachary Hooper with CBS Affiliate, Western Mass News.

ZACHARY HOOPER – CBS:

Thank you so much for doing this briefing and for taking my question. Why did the DPH advise you to consult with the CDC? Did you initially suspect a viral component or that the deaths were due to something contagious? Have you ruled out that possibility completely?

SUPERINTENDENT RAWLE BRUMMELL:

We consulted with the CDC as a precaution, given the close proximity of the deaths. However, at this time, the cause does not appear to be viral, no.

ZACHARY HOOPER – CBS:

At this time? Does that mean it still could, in fact, be traced to a virus?

SUPERINTENDENT RAWLE BRUMMELL:

Dr. Collins, would you like to address this question?

DR. ELLE COLLINS:

I'd be happy to. Although the CDC is still investigating the links between each victim, given the initial findings of blood serum tests, a viral component is not our initial conclusion, no.

SHERIFF'S OFFICE SPOKESPERSON:

Next question is from Melissa Mumby with the Boston Herald.

MELISSA MUMBY – BOSTON HERALD:

Hi, thanks for taking the question and for doing the briefing. Superintendent Brummell or Dr. Collins, could you explain, for the general public and also my editor, what is the take-away here? If it's not an infection, what possible explanation is there regarding why so many deaths occurred in the same neighborhood during the same 48 hours?

DR. ELLE COLLINS:

I understand your concern, and while we don't believe the link is communicable, the investigation is ongoing, so it would be irresponsible to give a formal assessment at this time. However, we do not believe there is an ongoing threat to the general public.

MELISSA MUMBY – BOSTON HERALD:

Have you found any connection between the victims other than their physical location?

SUPERINTENDENT RAWLE BRUMMELL:
Besides the victims knowing one another as neighbors, no, we have not. Next question.

SHERIFF'S OFFICE SPOKESPERSON:
Next is Angel Ortiz with the Associated Press. Angel, go ahead.

ANGEL ORTIZ – Associated Press:
Is it possible that something environmental caused the deaths, then, if all of the victims lived in the same immediate location? Soil? Gas lines? Water?

DR. ELLE COLLINS:
That's certainly a possibility, and we are looking into that.

ANGEL ORTIZ – Associated Press:
So, you are saying that the gas lines could be compromised? Or the water system? Is this a possible terrorist attack?

SUPERINTENDENT RAWLE BRUMMELL:
Dr. Collins did not say that, and I want to be clear that no one is implying terrorist activity. Next question.

SHERIFF'S OFFICE SPOKESPERSON:
Next is Jason Beale with—Sorry: what affiliate are you with?

JASON BEALE:
I am a freelance internet writer with contributions to Wikipedia, TheTruthisOutThere, and StatesWatchdog. Superintendent Brummell and Dr. Collins, you have both stated that the deaths occurred over a period of 48 hours. Does that time frame correspond with the snowfall of Winter Storm Mia? Is there a correlation between the storm and the deaths?

SUPERINTENDENT RAWLE BRUMMELL:

Sir, this is a formal briefing and open only to the press.

SHERIFF'S OFFICE SPOKESPERSON:

Please step aside and allow the next person to—

JASON BEALE:

I write for a number of online forums and have every right to be here. The public wants to know: did the snow kill these people? Is—Hey, get your hands off me! [unintelligible]

SUPERINTENDENT RAWLE BRUMMELL:

Next question.

Chapter Nine

Jackie Ketchum stared at her computer screen. She reread the short email from her new editor expressing his excitement at receiving her manuscript later that week. Then, she pulled up another window and glanced at the document's word count. 30,000. It was less than half of what she needed to get done by Monday morning.

She rubbed her eyes and ran a hand through her hair. Surely, she could sit her ass down, focus her mind, and grind out fifty thousand more words. She knew of a writer who had procrastinated so long on an upcoming project that he locked himself in his basement for two weeks, surviving on black coffee and whiskey as he produced what became one of his fans' favorite novels. Jackie thought a moment. She had plenty of coffee, but she had neglected to stop at the liquor store the day before and freshen up her supply of spirits. How could anyone expect her to write without a few vodka rocks?

"Madness. Am I right, Jimmy?" Jackie asked the fat orange cat reclining on the rug nearby. Jimmy said nothing in return. Instead, the cat rolled onto its back and stretched its front legs far above its head, watching Jackie warily out of the corner of its eye. "Don't worry: I know that trap. No belly rub for you, tiger," she said.

Jackie stood and walked to the full-length mirror at the end of her hall, examining herself. She was developing dark circles under her eyes. Crinkles of age had formed around the edges of her mouth. After only four decades on this earth, her body was beginning to break down, oxidize against its environment like a copper statue. It all seemed fitting: after nearly twenty books, her creativity had begun to ossify as well.

She rubbed her eyes again and leaned closer to her reflection. Her eyes were bloodshot from staring at the glare of a computer screen for hours. It was well into the afternoon. She had started writing at nine in the morning and managed to knock out two hundred, maybe three hundred words. At this rate, she would be done with the book sometime around next Christmas.

She needed a change of environment. Fresh air. She walked quickly to the window overlooking her driveway. The landscaping and plow service she contracted to keep her property neat and tidy was finishing its last run down her walk, sprinkling a heavy-handed dose of ice melter atop the surface they'd scraped almost bare. The storm had quieted but hadn't come to a complete halt; flakes continued to drift from the sky, delicately dotting the strips of exposed blacktop.

Jackie shoved her feet into a pair of boots and put on her coat. The landscaping team had packed up their equipment and was on its way down the street. She grabbed her wallet from its makeshift home on top of the microwave and her keys from the hook by the door and checked the time. Two thirty. The Packie, the liquor store a block away from Whistler's, was certain to be open by now.

In her distraction, she didn't notice as she opened the

door to her breezeway the cat shuffling next to her or his sly escape onto it, so when she opened the outside door and an orange blur darted past her, it took her a moment to understand what had happened.

"Jimmy!" she called as he maneuvered cautiously around the hibernating rosebush and along the front of the garage. "Jimmy! Come back!" On hearing her voice, however, the house pet increased the velocity of its run and scampered over the fence and into Jackie's backyard. Its bright orange coat disappeared from view in the snow drifts.

Jackie turned back and walked through the breezeway and out the door to the yard. She started down the cement steps and found her calves swallowed by the foot of snow. She took two more hesitant steps. The wind blew her hair into her face. Snow crept over the tops of her boots and surreptitiously climbed inside. "Jimmy!" she cried, but her voice faltered on the last syllable.

Walking in an exaggerated but careful stride, Jackie made her way into the center of her backyard, looking intently for any sign of Jimmy. She turned toward the fence. The wind shifted suddenly, spraying a gust of snow that pelted her face like hard grains of salt. She called out for the cat twice more, then stopped to listen. Something cried back near the fence. Was it a faint meowing?

The frigid air whipped over her cheeks once more, whistling softly as it tousled her hair. The faint sound repeated, but this time, Jackie could not pinpoint from which direction it came. She walked toward the fence, her eyes peeled for any sign of her wayward pet, but when she reached the boundary, there was no sign of him. The indistinct crying began again, chiming softly from the other side of the yard. Jackie stood very still and listened carefully. Within the sound came a series of words, unintelligible over the rushing tintinnabulation of the wind. Someone was speaking fast, she thought, but in a mournfully ominous manner. Who?

In the corner of her eye, a hazy orange shape slinked by. Jackie turned and looked over the fence. Jimmy was on the driveway once more. He glanced back at his owner, folded his ears back as if preparing for a predator's attack, then high-tailed it toward the road and down the sidewalk. Jackie watched him helplessly, then sighed. The cat would return when he was good and ready, she decided. It was bitterly cold outside: he would be waiting for dinner by the time she was back from her errand.

She backtracked through her original footprints as best she could, but by the time she made it to the cement stairs and out to the garage, her socks were wet, and with each step, a slight squish leaked out from between her feet and the soles. She slid behind the wheel of the Subaru, not bothering to let the engine warm. It would be a quick trip, she thought. A few bottles of vodka, maybe a bag of pretzels, and right back home.

The road had been plowed hours earlier, and the car shimmied a bit as it powered forward in the ruts. Jackie had never gotten used to driving in bad weather. Even rain made her a little uneasy. She gripped the steering wheel tightly and felt her spine tense as the street sloped downward and she prepared for the car to slide. She passed Carol and Rose's house on her right. Framed by one of the second-floor windows, Rose stood staring down at the street. Jackie lifted her hand from the wheel just long enough to give a curt wave, but Rose did not seem to see her. Instead, the old woman continued to stare intently at the snow-covered road and the house beyond it.

When she turned onto the road for Whistler's and the liquor store, Jackie was surprised to find it hadn't been plowed. It appeared that a few intrepid drivers had muscled through the deep snow and down the street recently, leaving tire tracks for Jackie to follow, but after a few feet, she stopped the car. She didn't want to get stuck halfway down the road and the walk would do her good. She turned off the engine and climbed out.

A pink neon sign advertising a brand of wine Jackie had never heard of glowed in the front window of The Packie, sidled by a full color poster advertising menthol cigarettes. In the ad, two very blonde women with thick white teeth laughed hysterically at a man juggling nearby. Jackie didn't know what any part of the tableau had to do with smoking, but she supposed that was how media worked: Trick the watcher into thinking he was seeing one thing when all along, it's really another.

The temperature inside the liquor store seemed almost tropical compared to the outside. The windows glistened with sheets of condensation. Behind the counter, a handsome Pakistani man holding a beaten paperback nodded at her, visibly unsurprised that the weather—or treacherous road conditions—hadn't kept his most frequent customers from stopping by. Jackie had asked him one evening, just making polite conversation, if his location just a few doors down from a bar impeded his sales.

"Just the opposite," the man replied, sliding Jackie's purchase into a thin paper bag. "We close two hours before Whistler's. Every evening, like clockwork, fifteen minutes before I lock up, I get two or three customers, stocking up for after last call." He handed her the bag. "Some people never want to be without a drink."

Jackie smiled politely, but she felt her face flush a bit. The beer-themed clock on the wall behind him displayed 10:35 p.m..

The Pakistani man focused his attention back on his book. Jackie slipped to the back of the store, eying the refrigerator cases of beer, then the various shapes and sizes in bottles of bourbon and scotch on the nearby shelf. George

Thorogood whispered an earworm of a song chorus into her head. She thought of her neighbor Steve, how he was always humming a classic rock tune whenever she visited the bar, even if something contemporary were playing on the jukebox. As Jackie did so, as if summoned, Steve emerged suddenly from around the corner of the aisle and nearly bumped into her.

"Hey!" he exclaimed, "Fancy running into you."

"Literally," said Jackie. "Whistler's open today, even with the storm?"

Steve smiled. "Well, you know," he said, "it will be slow to start off, but people get cabin fever pretty quickly. After the hurricane hit last year? Those two days without power? When we finally got the lights back on, we damn near broke the fire code." He wiped the top of his face with the wool hat he clutched in his hand. "I don't think I've seen so many disgruntled husbands and exhausted moms in one place at the same time."

"You're performing a public service," Jackie said. "Preventing mass suicides and family annihilations."

Steve stared at her blankly, and Jackie shifted uncomfortably. Finally, a broad smile crept across his face. Something about it gave Jackie an uneasy feeling in her stomach.

"So," Steve said, nodding at the bottles on the shelf in front of them. "Picking up some party supplies?"

Jackie shrugged. "Or a muse. Either one is welcome in my home right now." She picked up a bottle of Maker's Mark and pretended to examine the label. Steve's eyes were hyper-focused on her, and it was making her mind race. There was something off about his mannerisms, something slightly sinister. Had she done something to make him angry? What had she—and then, she remembered. "Oh my goodness," she said, replacing the bottle on the shelf and placing her hand on his arm. "Are you okay? Last night...I tried to stop and ask if you were hurt, but—"

Steve stared at her blankly again, then a look of recognition washed over his face. "Oh, right!" He laughed. "I barely felt it—it was just a bump, really."

Jackie frowned. "Are you sure? I mean, I felt the car hit you. I—" She stopped. What was she doing? If he says he is fine, he is fine, she told herself. Why try to convince him otherwise? "Well, I'm glad you're okay," she said. "You scared the bejesus out of me, running across the street like that." She thought of Steve, the image of him through her windshield, his shirt unbuttoned and flying behind him in the wind. Then, she looked at him carefully. His eyes were bloodshot: so bloodshot that he looked severely ill, like one of the shuffling sick on the zombie apocalypse TV show she used to watch. She eased slightly away from him.

"Yeah," Steve replied. "I'm dressed more appropriately now: that's for certain." He laughed again: a short, low chuckle. Then he clapped his hands and began to rub his palms together as if to warm them up for an important activity. "What are we picking up?"

Jackie moved further down the aisle and turned the corner. "Just a bottle of Tito's." She walked down the next aisle, scanning the rows of clear alcohol. A part of her hoped that her neighbor didn't follow her, but sure enough, as soon as she reached down to pick up a bottle, he appeared by her side again. She moved quickly to the end of the aisle and began to walk toward the cash register. "Are you working today?" she asked him over her shoulder.

Steve skipped quickly to catch up with her. "I'll be at Whistler's later," he said cryptically. "I was feeling a little stir-crazy myself, so I headed out for a walk." He watched Jackie pay for her purchase, then followed her silently out the door. Once they were outside, he added, "Think I could catch a ride home?"

Jackie shielded her eyes from the winter sun, then stepped one foot back in the tire track she had followed.

"Sure, Steve. My car's right over here." The two walked single-file in silence. Jackie felt her spine stiffen with trepidation. *It's Steve, dummy*, Jackie scolded herself. *He's not going to hurt you. This isn't one of your novels.* She laughed out loud at this. Steve was acting strangely, but she had seen him do some questionable things when he was tanked in the past. Maybe he was high, or even drunk. *Or maybe the storm is getting to him.* This odd notion hit her, sudden and violent, and she stopped in her tracks. Why would she think the *storm* was affecting him? Jackie brushed the idea aside and began to walk again. It was simply that her mind was taxed: the pressure of the book was bearing down on her, she told herself.

"Hey," Steve called from behind her.

Jackie turned around. Steve was pointing in front of her at her Subaru on the side of the road. In the short time she had been in the store, wind gusts had buried the front left tire and bumper in a snow drift. "Looks like we'll have to dig you out first," Steve said. "You got a shovel in your trunk?"

Jackie thought a moment. "Er, I don't even have a spare in there," she admitted sheepishly. When Steve raised an eyebrow at her, she shrugged. "I bought it as a rebuilt salvage. I don't drive very far, and I could pay cash." She laughed. "Be happy it has brakes, man."

They continued to walk until they reached the car. Steve stood staring at the bank of white smothering the front of Jackie's car, his hands on his hips. Flakes swirled around him, batting his face. A few stuck to his eyelashes. "I think I can rock her out," he said finally. "Give me the keys."

He held out an open palm. Jackie hesitated, then relinquished her car keys to him. He was a better driver than her, drunk or sober. "You need me to push or anything?"

Steve opened the door, then clicked the unlock button inside. "Nah," he said, sliding into the driver's seat. "Get in.

Let me see if all those Sundays of NASCAR on the bar TV deposited any knowledge."

Jackie walked to the other side of the car, opened the door, and climbed inside. "I don't think I've seen any races in the snow. You sure you don't mean the Winter Olympics?"

Steve started the engine. "Maybe after this, you can grab a broom and we'll do a little curling, too."

Lukewarm air screamed from the dashboard vents, and Jackie reached down to the controls and turned the indicator to DEFROST. Another whooshing sound ensued, and Steve turned on the wipers to clear the windshield. "Here goes nothing," he said, gently pressing the accelerator. The car moved hesitantly forward, its gentle push against the snow emitting a series of squeaking crunches. Steve hit the brakes, shifted into reverse, and backed the car up a foot. The snow reiterated its muffled, crackling protest, and Steve shifted back into drive and repeated the process twice more, inching a bit further forward each time. At last, he was able to turn the car around and drive back up the street and onto the nearby crossroad that had only a short layer of new snow lying atop it.

Jackie sighed with relief. "Ugh, I thought we'd be hoofing it back. Thanks for doing that."

Steve smiled but did not take his eyes off the road. "It's a good thing I was here, Jacks." He pressed his foot harder on the accelerator, and the car picked up speed. When they reached the turn for their side street, he did not slow but instead continued up the main road.

Jackie turned her head, watching the half-covered street sign grow smaller in the small streak of clearing in the snow-covered back window. "Where are you going?" She asked, her question ending in a small squeak. She looked back at Steve. The smile had not moved from his face. He continued to stare forward and pressed harder on the pedal. The speedometer's needle inched higher. 40 miles per hour. 45.

50. 55. Jackie gripped the inside of the door. She glanced at the road through the windshield. Bits of blacktop peeked here and there through the snow that had been flattened by a recent plow's blade. No other cars were on the road. A few intrepid shovelers, their heads buried in thick hats and hoods, moved slowly along their sidewalks or driveways. The whirring growl of snow blowers echoed down the street.

60.

65.

70.

"Steve!" Jackie screamed. "Please! Please slow down!" An intersection, its traffic light glowing a menacing red, raced toward them. Jackie let go of the door and grasped Steve's arm with both hands. "Please!" she begged. "Please, please stop!"

Steve's smile grew wider. Jackie could see the edges of his teeth, the point of a bicuspid peeking out from behind his lower lip. "Remember when you came in last August?" he said, his voice strangely calm. "For your birthday?" He pressed his foot harder on the pedal.

Jackie felt her mouth open, but no sound came out. She willed herself not to look at the approaching intersection, afraid of what she would see there, but Steve's expression was beginning to scare her even more. "Steve," she said finally, her voice a hoarse whisper. "Please don't do this. Please: you're scaring me. Steve, you're scaring me."

He turned to look at her. Steve pivoted his whole head so that he was looking at her straight on, even as the car continued to race furiously forward at a faster and faster pace. He was still smiling, but then, he tilted his head so that his forehead almost touched Jackie's. The shit-eating grin still plastered across his face, Steve lowered his voice. "It's a put-on," he whispered softly.

Then, he winked.

Jackie frowned, her mouth still twisted in a horrific plea. "What?" she asked, confused. "What did you say?"

Steve began to speak again, but as he did so, the car slammed into a utility pole, its front end crushing into an origami sculpture of metal and hoses and black paint. Jackie closed her eyes and felt someone bludgeon her forehead with a hammer. A stone hammer, one of those deals from a mythological god or fantasy novel, something wide and solid, she thought. It hit her flesh, then ripped through it, embedding itself in her skull, pushing her eyes far back behind her brain, her nose collapsing into a concave chasm and her teeth breaking off at the root and scuttling down her throat.

In the final moments before she slipped silently into the darkness, she realized that it hadn't been a hammer at all, but the steering wheel. The Subaru's horn cried out exasperatedly from somewhere in front of her.

And, alone in the car, Jackie's lifeless body let its foot fall lackadaisically from the gas pedal and onto the floor.

Chapter Ten

Kim O'Dell watched the tiny beads of minced garlic sizzle noisily in the layer of oil. She tilted the cutting board and scraped the pile of chopped onion on top of it, then sliced open the plastic wrapper surrounding the ground beef. She refused to touch the uncooked meat with her hands, and instead pulled chunk after chunk from the mound with a fork and dropped them in the pan, mashing the tiny snakes of pink and gray into hash. She perused the carefully measured ramekins of spices lined up along the counter and added their contents one by one. Chili powder. Chopped jalapeño pepper. Cayenne pepper. Mexican oregano. Cumin.

She stirred the fragrant concoction silently, watching the oil glisten over the browning hamburger. The image of the greasy man with the hairy hand, the dream man, reaching across the table to touch her flashed across her memory. She shook the colander of kidney beans and chopped tomato on top of the concoction, smothering the popping sounds and the unpleasant memory.

An orchestra of snow blowers purred from somewhere nearby. Kim glanced out the side window. Tom stood with his hand on his hip, the last remnants of the storm leaking from the sky and sticking to his blue New England Patriots hat. Tom was talking intently to someone, but from her vantage point, Kim could not see who it was.

The mixture in the pot began to bubble, and Kim stirred it thoroughly then covered the container with a lid. The clock on the microwave showed 3:10. She lowered the burner to allow the chili to simmer, then walked into the nearby dining room to peer out one of the windows there. Tom remained in the same position. He nodded his head emphatically to Dan, who stood a foot away from her husband, his back to Kim.

Without warning, everything in the house silenced. The lights in the kitchen went dark. Even the subtle hum of the refrigerator suddenly muted itself. After a beat, Aaron and Dylan began to bleat at Kim from the living room.

"Mom!"

"Power's out!"

"Is it gonna be back on soon? Ma? Is Dad gonna fix it?"

"I was right in the middle of a police chase. Fuck!"

"You were about to die anyway, pussy."

"Who's a pussy?!"

Kim inhaled slowly, then called out to them. "Boys! Language!" The two had been camped out on the sofa playing video games since leaving the breakfast table. From their constant commentary, Kim guessed the game was one of those shoot-em-up, role-playing things she had begged Tom not to buy them.

"They're boys," Tom had replied. "They are going to play them at their friends' houses anyway." Despite her protests, an array of violent car chase and street fighting games had appeared under the tree the previous month, and by Christmas afternoon, her teenage sons were yelling, "Kill that prostitute and take her money!" at the screen while she scrubbed holiday dinner plates and assembled them neatly in the dishwasher.

Aaron plodded loudly into the dining room and stopped when he saw his mother. "Why is the power out?" he asked, his tone suggesting that if the explanation were not satisfactory, he would throw a temper tantrum. He ran a hand through his mop of teenaged hair. A wave of unwashed boy —gym socks, testosterone, and rancid body spray—wafted across the room to Kim's nose, and she wrinkled her face in response.

"Dinner will be ready in a few hours. Why don't you go take a shower?" she coaxed.

"In the dark?" Aaron asked.

Kim glanced at the window. "It won't be dark for another hour. Leave the blinds open and put a flashlight on the sink."

Aaron sighed dramatically, and Dylan walked in and stood beside him. "Is the power going to come back on soon?" her younger son asked.

"I don't know," Kim said. "Maybe a power line came down with the weight of the ice on the lines. It might be a bit before the electric company can get to it." She looked out the window. Dan was no longer there, and Tom was carrying a shovel and walking toward the road. After a few seconds, he was out of view. A loud rumble signaling the passing of a city plow truck echoed across the silent house and petered out as the vehicle sped away down the hill.

Dylan stomped his foot lightly, like a small child. "Mom, what are we going to do without electricity?" he whined.

"Like I told your brother," said Kim, "you should go upstairs and take a shower. Get ready for dinner. We're having chili." When at this, Aaron crossed his arms in front of his chest, and Dylan rolled his eyes, Kim added, "Or you can go outside and help your father. He needs to clear the driveway and the snow blower's starter is still broken."

Defeated, both boys turned and headed toward the carpeted stairs. The sound of gangly legs stomping feet to the second floor reverberated loudly, followed by the creak of the bathroom door and the hum of the shower faucet. Kim continued to look outside. The afternoon sun had fought valiantly against the last vestiges of snow, but it sat low in the sky. Soon, the temperature would drop and anything that had managed to melt would refreeze overnight.

The sudden clamor of the back door opening and shutting made her jump, and she was surprised to see Tom walk into the dining room, still wearing his winter boots and coat. "Tom!" Kim said, looking at her husband's feet. The snow stuck to the sides of his ankles and calves was sliding onto the clean hardwood floor. "Tom, take your boots off. Give me your jacket."

She began to walk toward him, but he waved her away. "I got it. I'll hang them in the front hall to dry," he said and continued walking into the living room, a trail of dirty slush and sodden water in his wake.

Kim followed behind him. "But the driveway—" She glanced outside again. The sidewalk was only half-shoveled, and the driveway hadn't been cleared at all. "Tom, aren't you going to finish before dinner?" Her eyes flitted to her neighbor's walk, the driveway across the street. Carol, the schoolteacher, was standing alongside her snow blower, staring intently at something in her yard. Kim could see that her walk had been cleared down to the pavement, but the woman's driveway was still covered in snow. "I don't understand," Kim began. "Why—"

Tom emerged from the front hall. He was no longer wearing his wet coat or boots, but the Patriots cap remained on his head. A drizzle of melted snow slithered onto his cheek, but he seemed not to notice. "I have to get some work done," he said curtly, pushing past his wife and heading toward the kitchen. "I'll be in my office."

"But Tom, the boys might have school tomorrow," Kim said. "The driveway still needs to be shoveled, and—"

"Don't bother me," Tom instructed. "I'll probably be working late into the night."

Kim crossed her arms over her chest and followed behind him. "I made chili. Want me to bring you a bowl?"

"No," Tom replied gruffly, not looking at her. "I told you: don't bother me. I'll heat up the leftovers if I'm hungry later." He started up the stairs. One wool sock had gone rogue and was halfway off his foot as he climbed, but he did not stop to adjust it. When he reached the top of the stairs, he paused, half-turning toward his wife. "Kim, please. Don't..." His voice faltered. Kim saw his Adam's apple bob and heard him clear his throat. "Don't come in and talk to me, okay? Just...stay away."

Kim frowned, confused. Tom continued walking down the upstairs hallway, and a moment later, Kim heard the door to his study slam shut. She took one hesitant step forward, then rethought it and turned back toward the dining room.

She was gathering a handful of paper towels to clean up the trail of melted snow Tom had left on the floor when her cell phone trilled. Glancing at the caller ID, she grimaced then answered, a cheerful expression purposefully plastered across her face despite no one being there to see it. "Hi, Mom," Kim said, squatting to mop up the mess. "Did you fare okay in the storm?"

Tom's mother's voice was shrill in the tiny cell speaker. To be fair, it was shrill in person. "Fine, fine," she said. "It barely touched us. Mostly rain. But you know how Richard is: he was out there with the ice melter at dusk yesterday. He covered the sidewalks with it. Big chunks of blue rock salt, everywhere. Such an eyesore."

"Better safe than sorry, I suppose," Kim said. "But—"

Tom's mother continued as if Kim hadn't spoken. "At

least he bought the pet friendly kind this time. You know how the neighbors get with their dogs!" Her voice shrieked at the end like a smoke detector.

Kim crawled into the living room, dragging the cluster of towels along the remnants of water, the phone balanced against her ear. She looked back at the trail she had finished wiping and could see streaks on the natural stone in the kitchen from whatever dirt and grime had hitchhiked onto the snow Tom had trekked into the house. They had paid through the roof for that flooring: she would have to do a full mopping job.

"Patricia?" she called politely into the receiver, trying to edge in a word over her mother-in-law's chatter. "Patricia? Mom?" Kim stood up quickly, and in her haste, the phone fell from her shoulder and dropped noisily onto the floor. *That should get her attention*, Kim thought, but when she replaced the phone at her ear, she discovered the woman continuing to drone on about yard upkeep and winter weather woes. "MOM!" Kim finally yelled, and Patricia's yammering stopped abruptly. "Is everything alright?" Kim continued, her voice softer. "I am just getting dinner started and Tom is—"

"I was just calling to talk to Tom about his father's convertible. We've decided to garage it at the Cape this year, drive it down in March when the cold lifts, and Richard had some questions about the carburetor or some such thing. You know how men are," Patricia explained.

Kim didn't, but she found herself inexplicably nodding as she replied, "Uh-huh. Okay."

"I tried Tom's cell but he didn't pick up," his mother continued. "That's why I'm calling you, Kim. Is Tom there?"

Kim glanced at the stairs. "He probably left his phone in his office. He's outside shoveling right now. Why don't I tell him to call you when he comes inside?"

For a long moment, Tom's mother was silent. Then, after

an audible breath, she said, "Well, yes, fine. That will be fine. Have him call me when he gets in. Or after dinner. What is it you said you were making?"

"I didn't," Kim said, sharper than she intended. "Chili. I baked cornbread this morning." She opened the utility closet and pulled out the mop and bucket.

"Well, that sounds just yummy, Kim," Patricia said, her tone slightly condescending. "And very appropriate, what with the weather being so cold and damp. I'm sure the boys will love something spicy to warm them up."

Kim sniffed. "Yes, well, I hope so." She leaned the mop handle against her shoulder and stopped at the stove to stir the pot. "I'll make sure Tom gets back to you," she added, thinking of her husband standing at the top of the stairs, the winter hat dripping water along his face. *Don't come in and talk to me. Stay away.* "If not tonight, then first thing tomorrow."

When at last she was free of her mother-in-law, Kim placed the mop bucket into the kitchen sink, squeezed a stream of floor cleaner into it, and turned the faucet to warm. She told herself that Tom was likely stressed about something at work, that the weather may have caused a hiccup in one of the company's plans. She shouldn't take his abruptness personally.

She glanced outside at the driveway still covered in a blanket of white.

Tom knew what was best, Kim told herself. A single rogue snowflake danced along the wind and stuck itself to the windowpane, pausing for just a moment before melting into a fat droplet of water and streaming in a thin rivulet down the glass.

Marked Increase in Suspicious Deaths During Snowfall

Source: Jason Beale, States Watchdog.org
Last update: January —, 20— 8:37 EST

Top Ten Snowiest States	Average annual snowfall, November- March, past decade	Percentage of deaths labeled suspicious/unexplained, April - October	Percentage of deaths labeled suspicious/unexplained, November – March
New Hampshire	102.3 in	2.7%	5.1%
Maine	93	2.2%	4.7%
Vermont	83.2	1.5%	3.3%
Alaska	80.6	3.0%	6.4%
Wyoming	77.47	1.8%	3.6%
New York	71.3	2.9%	4.8%
Michigan	70	3.9%	8.7%
Massachusetts	62.2	2.0%	5.8%
Minnesota	58.9	2.6%	4.3%
Utah	57.2	1.0%	3.2%

Chapter Eleven

Carol Bennett pushed the start button on the gas-powered snow blower and carefully angled it out of the garage and down the perimeter of her driveway. When she was almost at the street, she heaved the handles to the right and did her best to swing the heavy machine so that it angled down the sidewalk. The rubber grips vibrated forcefully beneath her gloved fingers, though the whir of the motor was muffled. Her wireless earbuds streamed The Yeah Yeah Yeahs' *Fever to Tell* album into her brain, and all ambient noise was further muted by a pair of fuzzy earmuffs atop them.

The snow was heavy, and it took some effort to push the blower through it, even with fueled propulsion. Across the street, her neighbor Tom brushed a layer of snow from the top of his mailbox and slowly cleared a path down his front stairs. When he reached the bottom, their neighbor, Dan, appeared from around the corner of his own house. He scanned the street, pausing for a long moment to look at Carol, who nodded politely. Dan only stared back blankly before turning his head toward Tom and walking woodenly toward him.

Carol concentrated on keeping the blower straight as it powered through the foot and a half of packed snow. The dilatory sun drooped low in the sky, slowly easing itself back to bed. Its marigold yellow glare temporarily blinded Carol when she tilted her head back, a delicate sprinkle of snowflakes eddying about the air and brushing down her cheeks.

What had her mother been signing when Carol pulled her back from the shed in front of that woman? *Hiding in there. It wants to come out.* Carol simply nodded, a part of her embarrassed for Rose to be caught by a stranger acting so erratically. *I can hear it hiding in there.*

Hear it. Rose had chosen that word. Earlier that morning, when Carol mentioned the incoming weather, she had gotten the same response. *Yes, I heard it.* Her mother had been born deaf and had refused to even consider the cochlear implant her doctor once suggested. Maybe, Carol thought, her mother meant that she felt it, that she had sensed something rumbling inside of the shed or discerned the drop in barometric pressure that indicated an oncoming bout of wet weather. As a teenager, Carol never turned the stereo in her room higher than a whisper unless she was wearing headphones. If she did, her mother would be at the door, pounding her fist against the frame to tell her daughter to lower the volume. It was just her luck to have a deaf mother who was so attuned to the molecular structure of the air that she was agitated by vibrations of sound.

Then what had been *hiding*? And what, Carol thought, a trickle of unease returning, wanted *to come out*?

Carol turned the snow blower 180 degrees and slowly cleared the other half of the sidewalk. The sun was at her back, and she could see Tom and Dan were embroiled in an intense discussion across the road. Tom removed his bright blue winter hat and squeezed it between his hands, a makeshift stress ball. When he repositioned it back on his head, Dan leaned in close to him, his mouth directly over Tom's ear, and said something that made Tom draw back. The latter stared at his friend for a long minute before he grabbed his shovel and began to walk away from Dan and down the sidewalk.

Carol looked back down at her snow blower's path. Karen O screamed that she could keep her black tongue, and Carol hummed along. She still had the driveway to clear, but her shoulders were starting to ache. Surely, school would be closed for another day if the snow continued to fall, however light. She had to take a break. She would finish the walk and return to the driveway tomorrow, she thought.

"Uh huh," Karen O agreed, repeating the affirmation over and over in time with Nick Zinner's rapid-fire 32nd notes on the guitar.

Carol continued pushing the blower along the sidewalk until both sides were clear. In her peripheral vision, an enormous plow truck lumbered along the street, pushing piles of snow into mountains along the perimeter of the road. The bottom of Carol's driveway would be nearly impassable by the time they returned the next day, a wall of slushy white speckled with dirt and gravel quickly hardening into a thigh-high enclosure. Her muscles cringed at the thought. She looked up at the house. Rose stood in the window, a heavy sweater wrapped around her shoulders. She raised a hand and waved timidly at her daughter, and Carol took one hand from the snow blower's grip and waved back. Only then did Carol realize that her mother was not motioning to her at all but to something behind her, something in the front yard. Carol looked around frantically but saw nothing, nothing but a smooth blanket of snow smothering her lawn and draping lazily along the tops of her bushes.

With a sigh that she felt in her chest rather than heard, Carol began to maneuver the machine back toward the garage. When she was almost at the entrance, another flash of movement darted to the side of her. This time, Carol turned to look.

Rose, her tiny frame swollen with layers of thick winter clothing, stood swaying at the fence opening to the backyard. As a stiff wind carried waves of white into the air, Rose's jacket hood trimmed in matted faux fur blew back from her head, and wild, colorless hair whipped around her shoulders. Before Carol could react, Rose turned and began trudging slowly toward the shed, her gait impeded by the firmly packed veneer of snow lying still untouched in the backyard.

Carol pulled off her earmuffs and tapped on the bottom of her earbud to silence it. She didn't bother to shut off the snow blower but abandoned it and ran quickly toward her mother, who was crouching slightly. She appeared to be motioning to something at the other end of the yard: something, Carol thought, near or inside of the shed. When she reached her mother, however, she didn't care what the reason was for Rose's expedition outdoors. The retrieval of her mother from the yard seemed to be playing on an unending loop.

Frustration seething inside her, Carol grabbed her mother by the shoulders and shook her hard. "What are you doing?!" she screamed, pressing her face only inches from Rose's. "Why the fuck are you doing this to me?! Huh? Tell me, for Christ sakes! Tell me why!" She ran her hands down her mother's arms and grasped hold of her wrists, jerking her forward, the slippery fabric of the overcoat trying desperately to shirk Carol's grip.

Rose stared blankly at her, her expression revealing nothing.

"Why?!" Carol screamed again. "I know you understand me! I know you do! Just tell me: why are you doing this?!"

* * *

A memory, clear as glass, resurfaced in Carol's mind. She was in second grade, at a classmate's birthday party. Carol's family had recently moved to the neighborhood, and she was surprised to find an invitation to the event on her desk at her new school one day after recess. The girl's name was Allison, and when she saw Carol open the pink envelope and pull out the card with the pattern of strawberries dotting the edges, she slid next to her. "Smell it," the girl instructed, and Carol lifted the card to her nose. A sweet berry-like scent wafted into her nostrils. "It smells like shortcake," explained Allison, "because that's my favorite dessert, and we're going to have it at my party."

"Okay," Carol replied, unsure of what else to say.

"You can buy me a record for a present," said Allison. And that's what Carol did. That afternoon, after showing the invitation to Rose, her mother accompanied Carol to the nearby Caldor and the two walked directly to the music section at the back of the store. The Top Ten releases that week stood in a special display, front and center. Carol selected the one with a blonde man surrounded by vacant turquoise outlines of himself on its cover, and Rose handed her the eight dollars, standing watch as her tiny daughter proudly handed the dollar bills to the big-boned woman behind the register.

It rained the day of the party, so the children sat indoors, around Allison's dining room table, eating fat chunks of angel food cake smothered in sugary strawberry sauce and whipped cream while Allison tore open gaily-wrapped twelve-inch squares, one after another: Sting, the Eurythmics, Paul Young, Prince and the Revolution, Dire Straits, Talking Heads, and Carol's selection, Howard Jones. When Allison saw what her new classmate had selected, she yelped with joy. "Oh my gosh!" she cried happily. "I wanted this one so bad! How did you know?"

Carol smiled sheepishly and felt her face blush. Allison

slid immediately from the table and pulling the shiny new LP from its sleeve as she ran, placed the record on the family's turntable and positioned the needle's arm atop one of the grooves. The girls listened to the entire album, both sides, singing what lyrics they remembered to the songs they recognized from the radio. When the last song was done, Allison stood next to Carol's chair and draped one arm around her shoulder. "We should be best friends," she said, and Carol, gobsmacked at her luck, nodded in agreement. Things really *could* get better, just like Jones sang in his song.

"Well," said Allison's mother, her hand resting on her hip, "it's too wet to play outside, so I got a movie from the video store. Head into the living room."

Twelve squirming girls piled into the sofa and chairs surrounding an intricately carved television cabinet, and Allison slid from her seat and pressed PLAY on the VCR. The movie was Disney's *Amy*, and the beginning lagged a bit, causing the squirming to increase in frequency until finally, a blond boy in tattered overalls appeared on the screen. "He's cute," one girl said, and the others murmured their agreement and paid closer attention. Carol, however, continued to squirm. The movie was about a school for the deaf, and the flick's heroine, Amy, was teaching the students how to speak. The deaf children didn't act like her mother, however. They flailed their hands wildly around, cried out in grunts and squeals like animals. Soon, the other girls at the party began to giggle at the actors' antics. They started to mimic the characters, jumping around and whooping like the monkeys Carol had seen once at the zoo. One of Allison's friends stood up and waved her arms around wildly like she were being electrocuted. Carol said nothing. She bit her lip, hard.

Finally, at the climax of the film, one of Amy's students ran out onto train tracks in the middle of the night and was subsequently run over. The girls erupted into a fit of uncontrollable laughter. Allison slapped the side of the couch hard. "Deaf people are so stupid!" she announced, and ten seven-year-olds giggled loudly in agreement. One seven-year-old sat like a stone, wishing she could be anywhere but at that birthday party, even if it meant she herself were under the wheels of the offending train.

Outside, a car horn honked. Allison's mother walked in front of the screen and to the picture window. "Someone's parents are here," she said. "Okay, girls, start gathering your things. Allison, say thank you to your friends."

Carol leaped from her corner of the sofa and ran to the window. A battalion of station wagons and sedans was assembling along the curb, her mother's wood-paneled Pinto among them. Carol scrambled to the mudroom and retrieved her jacket, then, without saying goodbye, ran out the door and down the cement steps to the sidewalk. Many of the parents had exited their vehicles and stood in pairs and trios, chatting together. Her mother stood alone next to the Ford's driver's side door. When she saw her daughter, she smiled. *Did you have a good time?* she signed as Carol approached. *Was the party fun? What did—*

Carol shot out her arms to block her mother from moving her hands any further. Rose frowned, confused. She pulled her hands away from Carol's and began to sign again. "Stop!" Carol yelled, looking up at her mother with the sternest expression she could muster. "Stop! Stop!" She grabbed her mother's hands in hers and wrenched them down to her sides. After a long moment, she let go and ran around the car and climbed into the passenger side. Rose watched her, her arms remaining still. When her daughter shut the car door, Rose slowly opened her own and climbed behind the wheel. Allison's party guests trickled from the house and joined their parents, all of them silently watching the Pinto as it pulled away from the curb and drove away.

"Why?!" Seven-year-old Carol shouted when her classmates were no longer visible in the back window, the tears she had held so tightly in Allison's living room now streaming uncontrollably down her face. "Why did you do that to me?! Why?!"

* * *

"Why?" Forty-six-year-old Carol repeated, this time barely a whisper. She let go of Rose's wrists and looked down at the ground before looking back at her mother. *Please come inside, Mom*, she signed, pausing to pull the earbuds from her ears and shoving them in her coat pocket. *Please. It's too cold out for you to be out here. I'll be inside in a minute.*

Rose pointed at the shed. *You don't understand*, she signed. *I saw—*

Carol held her hand up. *Please*, she repeated. *Please just come inside. Okay?*

Rose exhaled a long breath, then nodded her hand and entwined her fingers with Carol's. As they turned to begin walking toward the door, another gust of wind blew across them, methodically stirring the powdery top of the snow drifts and pulling it up into the air. For one long moment, everything surrounding mother and daughter was milky and opaque as if they had become trapped within a shroud. Cold air whistled across and into Carol's naked ears, and without understanding why, she glanced back at the shed. The weather had blown the snow into a skateboarder's half-pipe, a thin slice of white creeping up almost to the handle.

When they reached the door to the kitchen, Rose squeezed her daughter's hand and walked inside without argument. Carol stood a moment, watching her mother remove her heavy coat and boots on the other side of the window. Satisfied Rose wasn't going to go back outside, Carol turned and walked toward the driveway. She was surprised to see her neighbor standing behind the handles of the snow blower.

"You left it running," Jackie said, smiling. She motioned with her hand toward the control panel. "I didn't see you, so I was going to turn it off, but then I realized: I don't know how to work the damn thing." Jackie laughed nervously, but she kept her eyes trained on Carol.

"I'm sorry?" Carol said.

Jackie stopped laughing, but the smile remained. "I said, you left the snow blower running. No one was around, so I came over to at least watch out for people getting too close to the auger." She pointed at the wide intake grinder at the front of the machine. "That's where the snow is pulled in and pulverized. Might get a bit messy if a kid, or—God forbid—somebody's pet got sucked into the front." When Carol said nothing in return, Jackie shifted her weight back and forth between her feet. "You need any help clearing the snow? I pay a service to do mine." She motioned toward her house. "But maybe I could use the exercise."

"Oh, no," said Carol. "No, that's kind of you, but I can take care of it." She rubbed her ears. They were tender and felt strangely scorched, as if she had held her head too close to a fire and flames had licked it. Her earmuffs were missing. She scanned the ground around the snow blower but could not see them anywhere. "That reminds me. I appreciate your help the other night. You know, with my mother." She paused. "I'll be honest: I'm at my wit's end. I'm just not sure what to do anymore. She wanders..." Carol felt Rose's fragile wrists under her hands again, how tightly she had gripped her mother in anger. Her own mother.

Jackie took a step forward and reached a hand out. Carol thought she would rest it on her upper arm; instead, she covered Carol's left ear with her palm. Her hand was cold: icy, even. "I can't imagine how difficult it's been for you." She smiled again, but something about the expression didn't seem right. Her lips parted slightly, exposing a hint of teeth behind them, but the friendly expression stopped dead at her cheekbones. Her eyes shone glassy and hard, like a hungry predator fixed on its prey.

Carol pulled away. "I should put this away," she said, then steered the snow blower into the garage.

Jackie ran alongside her, jumping ahead and walking to the back wall. She put her hands on her hips and squealed excitedly. "Hey!" she yelled. "Look at that!"

Carol stopped pushing the machine and ran immediately to where Jackie was standing. "What?" she asked. "What's the matter? Do you see something?"

Jackie pointed at two beach chairs hanging on pegs. "I have the same set," she said. "The fabric is fantastic, isn't it? None of that scratchiness of the plastic woven kind. And no imprints of crisscrosses on the backs of your thighs when you stand up." She grabbed the chairs from the wall and opened them, one by one, positioning them so that they faced each other slightly. Before Carol could protest, Jackie sat down in one and patted the seat of the other. "Take a load off. You've been working all afternoon. Take a second and rest."

Carol sat down. The chair was comfortable, more comfortable than she remembered it being. Perhaps it was the extra layer of clothing she was wearing. More likely, it was the heavy weight of exhaustion she had been carrying for months. As she relaxed her legs, she felt that weight slip from its carrying case and tumble down her back, spilling onto the cement floor like a puddle of motor oil. Carol closed her eyes and tipped her head back.

"See?" Jackie said after a long moment had passed. She leaned backward in her chair. "What did I tell you? Things can only get better. Isn't that what Howard Jones said?"

"What?" Carol's head snapped back. She opened her eyes. "What did you say?" A wave of nausea suddenly washed over her, sloshing about inside of her head. "I don't feel very well," she said. Her voice sounded far away, slurred. An icepick of pain stabbed at her temples.

Jackie leaned sideways so that her mouth was nearly even with Carol's ear. Her breath was cold, colder than even her hand had been. Carol thought of the peppermint chocolate candy commercials from her childhood, the ones where spokespeople bit into the product and their breath fogged.

Jackie's breath continued to dance along her earlobe, the side of her neck. It felt refreshing against the strange wave of heat creeping up her torso. Very softly, her neighbor began to hum something familiar, nostalgic: the bridge to that Howard Jones song, the one Allison had gotten so excited over forty years earlier. *Whoa whoa whoa, whoa whoa, whoa-whoa-whoa.*

But—

An eclipse fell over Carol's vision. Everything around her darkened. Was it evening already? Carol looked toward the entrance to the garage, trying to gauge the time from how much sunlight remained, but the door was shut. When had she shut the garage door?

An incessant murmur droned from somewhere nearby. The snow blower. She never turned off the snow blower. How long had it been running inside the closed garage? Her thoughts jumbled together like a string of Christmas lights jammed haphazardly into a box one size too small. She tried to pull the wires apart but only succeeded in breaking a few of the bulbs.

Jackie tilted her head slightly and flashed the predatory grin once more. "Frost was right, wasn't he? With his Desert Places?"

Carol frowned. The world around her spun, tilted. The pain in her head shot into her chest, squeezing her lungs in a vice grip. She forced the words from her throat, and they stumbled drunkenly from between her lips. "What...are... you...What...do...you...mean...?"

"Those things that haunt you in the dark," Jackie said, her pupils growing wider until the blackness swallowed every speck of iris whole, "never stay hidden forever."

A volcano of hot bile erupted into Carol's throat, spilling from her mouth and nose. She gagged and tried to cough, but the heavy weight climbed back onto her chest, pinning her rib cage to the chair. Vomit plugged up her esophagus, smothering her like a thick, wet pillow.

Carol struggled to turn her body in a plea for help, but the chair beside her was empty.

Excerpt from:

Remembering the Great Thanksgiving Storm: Five Years Later

Ohio Lifestyle & Culture
vol. XXVI, issue no. 9
November 25, 1955

On the Saturday following the Thanksgiving holiday of 1950, the Ohio State football team took the field in their title match against Michigan. Within minutes of kickoff, the snowfall doubled, then tripled in intensity, causing near white-out conditions for the players, who slipped and slid along the ice-laden grass at Ohio Stadium until finally tumbling into a 9-3 loss. By the time nightfall arrived, the entire state was blanketed in a foot of freshly fallen snow, but the sister cities of Cincinnati and Columbus shook much of their snowfall at poor little Dayton, sitting midway between them, and the town's landscape became buried under drifts soaring five feet in height by Sunday. Residents lay trapped in their houses, and unlucky out-of-towners making their way home from the holiday found themselves dependent on the benevolence of Dayton residents when their automobiles ran aground and had to be abandoned on the sides of roads.

The city stood frozen; those businesses that opened despite the weather transformed into makeshift motels when impassable roads made employees' return home impossible. Department store shelves lay barren, their stock of wool sweaters, flannel shirts, and long underwear liquidated in a day's time. The National Guard patrolled the streets, delivering food to those hunkering and hungry.

The modest Colonial of Nathan and Maryann Cohn stood atop a steep hill over which a main thoroughfare normally teemed with traffic. That evening, however, Maryann stood watching the flakes as they drifted toward the window from dark skies when a young couple trudged up their walk, a pair of valises and a toddler in tow. Their car had become immobile at the bottom of the hill, they said, and without heat or food and no way for their relatives in the next town to retrieve them, they needed shelter. A half-hour later, another knock at the door followed, bringing a second stranded couple, and fifteen minutes after that, yet another small group—this one, an 80-year-old woman, her son, grandson, and three Labradors—inquired as well.

Despite their modest furnishings and little food for themselves, the Cohns offered sanctuary to every person who solicited help, and by midnight, their living and dining rooms were awash with the bodies of strangers who used couch cushions, table linens, and the Cohns' own bed pillows for comfort.

Exhausted and hungry, Nathan and Maryann folded a small blanket into a jelly roll to support their heads and curled up, clutching tightly to one another until morning. Maryann slid the lock on their bedroom door before retiring.

As the sun rose the next day, Nathan ventured into the front rooms of the house to tend to their house guests only to find them empty—barren of strangers, but also completely stripped of any furnishings. Someone had absconded with nearly all of their belongings not locked inside the master bedroom.

Nathan phoned the authorities and hours later, an officer arrived on a bulldozer to take their statement. No charges could be filed, however, despite the desolation on the first floor. There was no sign of a vehicle being stuck at the bottom of the hill. Furthermore, there were no footprints in the snow leading to or from the house. The deep blanket of white lay undisturbed, without even a single blemish.

Chapter Twelve

John Stephenson ran the faucet in the bathroom until the water was cold, then leaned into the basin and splashed handful after icy handful onto his face. He had spent the day on a merry-go-round of drowsy incoherence and sleep, and he scolded himself for taking too much of the narcotic. Now, his body felt fragile and hollow, his muscles weak, and his gait wobbly.

When he first awoke on the living room couch, John was confused. Out of habit, he checked the digital clock on the cable box, but it was black. John sat up. His stomach lurched a little, a side effect he knew was from sleeping too long without having eaten. After slowly pushing himself to standing, he wandered to the kitchen to check the microwave's clock. It, too, was dead.

He returned to the living room. A few lonely scrapes of shovels called out in the twilight. The snow piled in front of his house remained untouched save for a few intrepid footprints of passers-by along the sidewalk. John found his phone abandoned on the end table. He had forgotten to plug it in to charge and the battery read 10%. It was 4:40. He had been asleep for more than fourteen hours, and yet his body still felt exhausted.

Snippets of the previous evening flashed through his head. There had been a nightmare, something about his neighbors Janet and Dan, but he shook the mismatched puzzle pieces from his thoughts and walked to the side window to glance at his driveway. The snow there, too, was untouched.

John rubbed his chin, feeling the rough stubble scratch the underside of his hand. If the driveway wasn't cleared, deliveries wouldn't be made. Would he starve to death? If he did, how long would it take for someone to find his body? He didn't even have a cat to eat it anymore.

He glanced at his cell phone. He could call Louis, ask him to contact the plow service, but his ex's voice echoed immediately back.

John, it's time you started learning to do things for yourself.

Yes, I know that, John argued.

Then pick up the phone and call the service, the Louis voice responded. *Look at your neighbors' driveways: just about all of them are clear.*

Not all of them, John petulantly insisted. He looked outside again. Dan and Janet's driveway was untouched. He squinted and moved closer to the pane. In the growing dark, the layer of packed snow remaining after the city plows combed the road looked off, somehow. A dark stain permeated the expanse of white from the area between his and Dan's house. The odd streaks tapered off three houses down. Had they sanded? If so, why had they only dumped the sand in one concentrated puddle?

Suddenly, the light in the kitchen screamed to life. The microwave's tiny screen awoke and blinked to clear its eyes from sleep: 12:00. 12:00. 12:00. The refrigerator bucked and resumed its hum. In the living room, the cable box clicked, its red digital reading rolling through various configurations before finally settling on the correct time. John walked to his charging station next to the sofa and plugged in his phone. The illumination cast from the next room turned the front window into a faded mirror, and John's doppelgänger stared back at him, its facial features a dark blur.

Janet in the window. Naked. A knife against her throat.

John shook his head. He could contact the police, ask that they check on his neighbors, or better yet, he could call Louis and ask his advice, but he told himself what he had seen had been nothing but a vivid nightmare. The sleeping pills did that sometimes: made him dream fictional scenarios he would have bet his life had occurred. One evening, he awoke to find Louis curled up on his side, the top of his naked back sticking out from the tangled sheet. John grasped one shoulder and shook it wildly.

"What?" moaned Louis. "What? What is it?" He turned onto his back and rubbed his eyes, fumbling along the nightstand to grab hold of his alarm clock. "It's three in the morning," he said, his voice clearer. He placed the clock back on the table a little more forcefully than he intended. "What's the matter?"

"Your leg," John said, his voice only a hoarse whisper.

Louis sat up and pushed himself back toward the headboard so that he could lean against the pillows. "What about my leg? John, what are—"

John pointed to the lump of lower extremities beneath the covers. His hand was shaking. "Crushed," he managed to squeak out. "Gone. Your leg..."

Louis exhaled exasperatedly. "John, my leg is fine." He began to push the blankets down.

"No, No!" John yelled. He covered his face with his arms. "I don't want to see it!" The truth is, he *had* seen it: all of it. The two of them walking along a near-empty beach, the untouched sand smooth as glass, the sun's gaze so bright that the landscape appeared almost white. Louis turned to say something excitedly to John. As Louis walked backward in front of him, he spoke in such an animated way, was so energetically jovial, that John could not take his eyes from him. When the hole in the ground opened up behind him, it wasn't until Louis plummeted downward that John realized what had happened.

"Louis!" John yelled, leaning down into the crater. "Louis, are you alright?" He offered him a hand, and Louis grabbed it, but not before attempting to secure his foot into the side of the excavation and push himself up. Except— there was no foot to place. Below the knee, Louis' leg had been torn away, ripped from its joint. Strings of bloody pulp and sinew drifted down from the wound. As John watched, the excision point moved upwards. Louis' knee disappeared, then his lower thigh. Something was eating Louis' body away, an invisible entity devouring him, bit by bit.

John scuttled from the bed and rolled onto the carpet. He tried to slide his body under the bed frame but found that his stomach was just a hair too round. It took Louis a full hour to coax him from the floor and back into bed, and even then, John took great pains not to look down at Louis' legs.

Two months later, Louis was gone: not consumed by anything except perhaps his growing frustration at John's mental decline.

Are you taking your meds?

Louis' voice echoed in John's head, chiding him like he was a small child. It would be his first response to any wild story akin to the vision John recalled from the previous evening, and maybe it was justified. John ran a hand through his hair. The doppelgänger reflection stared back, and behind it, the neighborhood lulled into a staid hibernation for the evening. Under the bluish-black haze of the night sky, a dark figure resembling Carol Bennett crept quietly along the side of her house, stepped carefully across the deep desert of snow, and stood motionless in the shadow of the backyard shed, staring blankly up at Rose's second floor window.

Chapter Thirteen

Thursday morning, Kim O'Dell dumped the empty can into the kitchen trash and carefully printed *Endust* on the grocery list magneted to the refrigerator. As she washed her hands carefully in the sink, she watched the faint sprinkling of snow from the roof drift down past the window. After dumping more than a foot and a half on the ground, the storm seemed to have realized it had overstayed its welcome. It packed up its things and absconded north, leaving its discarded remains for the residents to clean up. Full sun awoke from its temporary hibernation, and its glare off the sparkling snow nearly blinded Kim as she anxiously scanned the untouched driveway.

Snippets of jeers and abbreviated curse words wafted from the living room. Instead of returning to bed after learning that school was canceled for another day, Aaron and Dylan set up shop after breakfast in front of the television to continue playing their drive 'em rob 'em kill 'em video game.

"I don't want to hear any of that language coming from either of you," warned Kim as they padded away from the table.

Aaron stuck a last slice of toast in his mouth. "Which language is that, Ma? French? German?"

Dylan gulped the last of his orange juice and slid the plastic cup on the table. "None of that Swahili business, Mom. Pinky swear." He burped loudly and followed his brother out of the room.

"Smart asses," Kim whispered. Would her kids be this cheeky if they were girls? Kim didn't think so. Or maybe they would be worse. She sprayed the table down with cleaner and scrubbed it thoroughly, then loaded the dishes into the dishwasher. Her husband had yet to make an appearance that morning. Tom had not emerged from his self-imposed quarantine in the study all night, not even to eat dinner. When Kim awoke that morning, he was still locked behind his keyboard, typing away.

The weather report predicted a significant warm up by noon; much of the snow accumulation would soften and melt, making it easier to move, but she had to at least shovel the knee-high piles away from the foundation. The last time they'd had a heavy rainstorm, water leaked into the basement. Even after a professional deep clean by a carpet company, Kim could still smell mildew in the cellar. Each time she ventured to the washer/dryer or chest freezer down there, she felt the spores sticking to the inside of her nostrils, burrowing into her mucous membranes, infecting her cells with filth.

"Aaron! Dylan!" she called. "Come help me shovel some of the driveway."

Her sons' ruckus abated for a long minute. Finally, Aaron called back, "Okay, Ma. Give us five minutes. We just want to get this mission done."

Kim sighed. She opened the refrigerator and pulled out the ingredients for the evening's dinner. Steaks. Lemon juice. Minced garlic. Worcestershire sauce. From the nearby cabinet she removed soy sauce, olive oil, Italian seasoning, and red pepper. She measured and blended the marinade, placed the steaks in a shallow dish, and poured the concoction over the meat. She covered the dish tightly with plastic wrap and placed it gingerly in the refrigerator to stew. In a few hours, she would remove the meat and cut it into smaller chunks, then return it to tenderize the rest of the afternoon. Tom could not resist steak tips; he was certain to take a break from work for dinner that night.

She wiped down the countertops with bleach again, then dug out her winter boots from the hall closet. "Boys!" she yelled, walking into the living room. "Come help me."

The two were splayed along the sofa, Dylan gripping a controller in both hands and staring at the screen, Aaron glancing back and forth between the television and his phone's screen. A miasma of morning breath and hormonal sweat hovered in the air. "Take a right," instructed Aaron. "Two streets up, toward the beach. There's a health packet and a bunch of weapons in that alleyway."

Dylan angled his body to the left as if leaning into a turn on a motorcycle. He swiveled his wrist and rotated the joystick with his thumb. "I see it. I see it." He straightened his body and leaned forward intently. The television emitted a ringing sound. "Got it! Fuck yeah!"

"Dylan!" Kim scolded. She crossed her arms in front of her chest. "Both of you. Your father is busy working, and that driveway has to be cleared. You really want your poor mother doing all the work herself?" As she said the words, a sick feeling curdled in her stomach. She sounded like Tom's mother. More importantly, when had she lost a connection with her own children? What kind of healthy, robust kid sits back and lounges away on the couch while his mom does back-breaking work?

Aaron looked up from his phone. "Mom, we'll help. Really. We—"

"We just want to finish this one thing," Dylan said.

"We'll be there in a sec. Promise." His eyes did not leave the screen, and he leaned his body in the other direction and continued to fondle the controller.

Kim walked past them and to the front hall. She retrieved her winter coat and gloves and walked back to the kitchen for her sunglasses, holding her breath until she was in the dining room. As long as the snow is away from the house, she told herself, the rest would take care of itself.

The air outside was colder than it appeared, but the persistent sun did its best to warm what it could. Icicles hanging above the home's entrance dripped sloppily onto the steps, forming round craters in the few inches of snow that had amassed since Tom had brushed them off the previous day. Kim looked around. It was Tom's habit to leave a shovel next to the back door during a storm for easy access later, but she didn't see one anywhere.

The snow on the driveway was already softening, and as she made her way to the garage, Kim's boot sank into it with a slushing noise. As she pulled the boot back, a soft smack reverberated from the ground beneath it. *Slush, smack. Slush, smack.* She had to sweep away with her foot the snow piled at the bottom of the door in order to open it, and already, a handful of the cold wetness migrated into her boots and tickled her feet. Inside the garage, the air was warmer, cozy even. The darkness smelled of dormant seasons: old dirt and grass clippings, raked leaves and pruned branches. Kim lowered her glasses and willed her eyes to adjust to the dark, and when she spied one of the smaller shovels hanging on a peg nearby, she grabbed it and brought it outside.

Snow was no longer falling, but drifts of it danced along with the wind. A strong gust carried a wave of white over Kim's face, and despite her sunglasses, she shut her eyes and waited for the horizontal surge of snow to abate. From the street, the faint echo of snow blowers purring and car tires squeaking combined into a dull hum. Someone's dog barked from far away.

Kim wedged the edge of her shovel against the side of her house and pulled the snow toward her, angling the pile she formed so that it tapered onto the driveway, the back patio, the side yard. She repeated the action again and again until a broad moat of grass and cement surrounded her house.

The snow blower's purr increased in volume.

The nearby dog stopped barking, then began again with more ferocity.

Another car shimmied noisily down the slippery road, sliding once, the driver regaining control by turning into the swerve, making the sedan appear to shake its hips in salsa dance.

Kim circled her house, clearing more of the snow, expanding the makeshift moat even wider. She had read somewhere that shoveling burned 400 calories an hour. She had eaten nothing for breakfast, consuming only a cup of black coffee, so she would go into dinner with a caloric credit under her belt. Restricting her meal to only steak and a single spear of asparagus, and she would be sailing on a keto wave, her carb consumption totals firmly planted in the black.

The snow blower cut its engine.

The dog barked a few more times, then stopped, embarrassed as a partygoer whose private conversation is broadcast to the masses when the music cuts out suddenly.

In the relative silence, a new sound emerged. This one sounded like metal sliding against metal. Kim stopped and listened harder. She had heard the sound recently although she could not place its origin. *Sloosh, clink. Sloosh, clink. Sloo*—that was it! Kim knew what it sounded like: a carving knife against a metal sharpening rod. Tom used one every time she served a roast or a turkey. In fact, he'd been using one—

The nightmare.

Kim pursed her lips and shook her head. She continued moving the snow further and further away from the house, concentrating on flexing her abdomen muscles. Bathing suit season would be here soon enough. No, she wasn't going to think about that stupid dream again. That's all it was: a dream. Still, she could still see her sons' mouths, dripping with saliva, the expression of satisfaction plastered across Tom's face as he bit into the chunk of her flesh he had excised from her foot.

Your marriage, your kids, your household. Consuming you.

The guilt is eating you up inside.

Sloosh, clink. Sloosh, clink.

It was then that she saw it: Tom's shovel. It stuck out of a snowbank in front of their property, as if her husband had placed it there temporarily while he went inside to pee or to grab a dry pair of gloves. She didn't remember seeing it on her last trip around the circumference of the house, but she hadn't been looking toward the street. Had he come outside while she was on the other side? If so, why had he abandoned the shovel? And where was he now?

She looked at her neighbor's sidewalk. Dan and Janet hadn't even begun to clear their snow away, which wasn't like them: they walked their dog religiously. Had they gone away for the week? Absconded in the middle of the night as the storm increased?

At the end of the street, where the road curved slightly, a bright blue ski hat poked out from a snowbank.

Kim turned back to the house and examined her work. Even if all of the snow melted in one day, which was highly unlikely, it didn't appear as though the water would run toward the house now. The driveway still needed to be cleared, but she might be able to bribe the boys to take care of it before dinner. She dislodged Tom's shovel from the snow mound and carried both implements to the back door. Aaron and Dylan could each grab one, then store them back in the garage when they were finished.

She kicked off her boots in the mudroom and carried her coat and gloves to the front hall, holding them close to her body to keep any errant snow from dripping onto the stone floor. The boys remained on the living room couch, Aaron holding the controller and Dylan acting as navigator. When they saw their mother walk into the room, twin looks of shame passed over their faces. "We're headed out there now, Ma," said Aaron quickly.

Dylan looked down at his phone, then at the television screen. "We'll finish whatever you couldn't do," he added, not looking at her.

"Great," said Kim, walking back into the dining room. "Shovels are by the back door. Dinner is at six, but it gets dark way before that, so..." She didn't bother to finish the thought, instead walking into the kitchen and removing the marinating steak from the refrigerator and setting it on the island's countertop. She squatted down to pull a large cutting board from the lower cabinet and as she rose, discovered Tom standing by the island, watching her with interest.

"What's for dinner?" he asked, peering down through the plastic wrap.

Kim delicately pulled back the cover to show him. "Steak tips." She retrieved an oversized cleaver and a sharpening rod from a nearby drawer and placed them side by side on the counter. "Would you sharpen this for me?"

Tom hesitated, then picked up both pieces. "Of course," he replied and began to run the blade along the rod's shaft. *Sloosh, clink. Sloosh, clink.*

Kim washed her hands, then carefully removed the steaks, still dripping with marinade, and arranged them on the cutting board. She held out one hand to her husband. "Scalpel, doctor?"

Tom smiled and placed the knife's handle carefully on his wife's palm. "Scalpel."

Kim held the meat firmly with her left hand and began to cut the first steak into two-inch cubes. "Where were you?" she asked without looking up. "Earlier, when I was outside. I saw your shovel."

Tom said nothing at first, then cleared his throat. "Oh, I must have left it there yesterday by accident. I'm surprised it didn't walk away."

Kim cut into the slab. "Oh, I'm not worried about that." She made another cut. "This is a nice neighborhood."

Tom laughed, a strange laugh, one that made Kim stop her cutting and look up at him. He was grinning at her, a wide, mischievous grin she last saw when he was talking about the sex club. "You were outside, then?" he said, the grin still fixed in place.

Kim looked back down at her work and made another cut. She pushed two cubes away from the steak and cut into the meat again. "Yes, I cleared the snow away from the house. I didn't want—"

"Did you hear it?" Tom interrupted.

Kim paused her cutting. "Hear what?"

"The snow."

Kim frowned. There was something in her husband's voice that set off an alarm in the back of her mind, something that was not entirely Tom. She picked up the cubes she had finished and placed them back in the pan of marinade. "What do you mean?" Kim asked softly, pulling another steak closer to her and making the first cut.

"I mean," Tom said, "did you ever really listen to the sound it makes? When it hits the ground. When it brushes up against the window. When it shakes loose from the tree branch and drifts down to the road."

Kim said nothing. She cut another cube, pushed it away with the back of the knife. Another cube, pushed away. Another. Another.

Tom leaned in closer and lowered his voice, the end of his sentence tapering down into a whisper. "It sounds, Kimmy, like *fingertips tapping on your flesh.*"

Kim's knife slipped. She steadied her hand and examined the oblong chunk of meat she had generated. It was decidedly smaller than the rest of the cubes and she would have to watch that it didn't overcook, but she threw it into the pan with the marinade. "That's an interesting comparison." She repositioned her knife and made another cut in the steak.

"I don't think you're listening," Tom said.

Kim made another cut. "Of course I'm listening." She began to feel a little light-headed. Another cut. All that shoveling on an empty stomach was catching up to her.

"Won't you come and join the party, babe?"

Kim wanted to look up at her husband, but something in his voice kept her eyes plastered to the meat. "Once I'm done making the cubes, I'll start working on the roux for the macaroni and cheese," she said, ignoring his question. Her head was swimming. She made another cut. "I'm going to steam some asparagus, too. How does that sound?" Another cut. Cubes in the marinade. A quick frame of darkness flashed across her vision. When she was done with the steak, she would sit down, rest a moment.

"You're not listening, honey."

Another cut. Another cut. Another cut. Another cut.

"I said," Tom hissed. "You're. Not. Listening!"

Kim looked up at him. Tom bent forward. He pressed both hands, palm-down, onto the countertop. His face was only inches from Kim's, and she watched as his mouth gaped slowly open and a thick string of drool poured from it and onto her right arm. She followed its journey with her eyes.

For a minute, she didn't understand what she was seeing, couldn't make sense of what was strewn about the white countertop.

Floating among the cubes of dark red steak in the pan of marinade were at least a dozen lighter-colored chunks, all of them wet with blood. She peered closer. One piece had a fingernail attached. On another, the curve of a knuckle jutted upward. Kim looked at her left arm, what remained of it. It had been crudely disarticulated a few inches below the elbow. A puddle of thick, dark blood pooled beneath it, streaming across the counter and drip, drip, dripping onto the floor below.

The new floor, Kim thought, dropping the cleaver with a clatter. *I'll have to get the mop.*

Once again, frames of darkness clicked across her vision. The room spun, and Kim felt her jaw crack and splinter as her head smashed against stone.

Excerpt, transcript from:

Bob Banderly's Science Central!

Children's Program
YouTube LiveStream

Episode 3.1   Aired Saturday, January —, 20— 9:00 ET

BOB:

Welcome back, kids! It's your old friend, Dr. Banderly, but you can call me Bob! With me as always is my good friend and neighbor, Mr. Muffins. How are you today, Mr. Muffins?

MR. MUFFINS:

I'm a sock puppet, Bob. I don't have feelings.

BOB:

Well, that's just great! I'm so glad you could join me for today's episode about something a lot of people are seeing first-hand this month: snow! Here in the northeast United States, we get a lot of snow, but did you know that every one of the United States can get snow?

MR. MUFFINS:

Even Hawaii?

BOB:

You betcha! In fact, in February 2010, all fifty states had snow on the ground somewhere within their boundaries. In Hawaii, only the highest elevations get snow, and in

161

February 2010, the Mauna Kea volcano had snow on its northern slope.

MR. MUFFINS:
What about Florida?

BOB:
Florida sees the occasional snowflake on its panhandle. That's the skinny part of the state in the northwest, kids. But in January of 1977, snow came down in the southern parts of the state, including West Palm Beach and Miami! Can you imagine? What would you do, Mr. Muffins, if you lived in Miami and saw snow coming down?

MR. MUFFINS:
I'd think I was having a stroke, Bob.

BOB:
Now, now, Mr. Muffins. Let's not scare our viewers with such talk. How about we investigate what snow is and why it falls?

MR. MUFFINS:
Sounds like a plan.

BOB:
In order for snow to form, the atmosphere needs two things: moisture and cold. When the temperature of the air is at or below freezing—

MR. MUFFINS:
That's 32 degrees Fahrenheit—

BOB:
or 0 degrees Celsius, and—

MR. MUFFINS:
Who the heck uses Celsius?

BOB:
Actually, Mr. Muffins, The United States and a few island nations are the only places in the world where the Imperial system is used. Everywhere else uses Celsius.

MR. MUFFINS:
Is this like an inches versus centimeters thing?

BOB:
Why, yes, sort of, but let's table that discussion for another day. When the temperature of the air is at or below freezing and there is enough moisture in the air, snow will form. The best temperature for snow to form is when the ground is between 15 and 40 degrees Fahrenheit. How dense or fluffy snow is depends on a lot of things, from the wind and weather conditions to the moisture level and temperature changes.

(Reaches below the counter and brings out a large handful of snow)

This is a snowball I collected from the last storm. I kept it in my freezer. What do you notice about it, Mr. Muffins?

MR. MUFFINS:
It's wet.

BOB:
Yes, and?

MR. MUFFINS:
(Rubs head on it) It's cold.

BOB:
Very! What else?

MR. MUFFINS:
It's white.

BOB:
That's correct. Most snow appears white because it reflects back most light. The amount of light a surface reflects is called its albedo. Do you know that word, kids? Let's say it together.

BOB and MR. MUFFINS:
Al-BEE-dough

BOB:
That's right. Albedo. Because clean snow's albedo is so high, it reflects white. But not all snow appears white. In parts of Canada and the Alps, fresh-water algae that thrive in cold weather grow on snow, making it appear pink.

MR. MUFFINS:
That's gross, Bob!

BOB:
Scientists call it watermelon snow. But you shouldn't eat it: the algae is a type of bacteria that could make you sick.

MR. MUFFINS:
Doesn't make it any less gross, Bob.

BOB:
What are you doing? Don't put that in your mouth.

MR. MUFFINS:
Why? The snowball isn't pink.

BOB:
Well, no, but let's not eat it. Let's talk about it instead, okay? Say, Mr. Muffins, what's the difference between a snowstorm and a blizzard?

MR. MUFFINS:
A snowstorm is when it snows heavily, but a blizzard must have high winds and reduced visibility. That means it's snowing so much you can't see in front of you.

BOB:
Why, yes, Mr. Muffins! How did you know that?

MR. MUFFINS:
I watch things besides this show, you know.

BOB:
Yes, but—

MR. MUFFINS:
A snow *squall* is a quick burst of snow, but a very heavy one. It's almost like a miniature blizzard. And—wait, shhhhh.
(Puppet rests its head against the snowball)

BOB:
What is it?
Mr. Muffins?

MR. MUFFINS:
Shhhh. Listen.

BOB:
I don't hear anything.

MR. MUFFINS:
(Picks up head) The crust on snow is when a hard top is formed by wind, rain, or melting sun, and beneath the crust is softer snow. Like a pie.

BOB:
Except don't eat it if it's pink.

MR. MUFFINS:
Or yellow.

BOB:
Graupel is the term used for when liquid droplets in a cloud attach themselves to ice crystals. The result is something that looks and feels like hail but is not as hard or dense.

MR. MUFFINS:
So, what's the difference between graupel, hail, and sleet?

BOB:
Good question! Graupel are snowballs with thin layers of ice around them. Hail is frozen raindrops: raindrops that turn into ice drops. Hail often occurs usually during a thunderstorm. Sleet is rain that freezes before it reaches the ground.

MR. MUFFINS:
This is an awful lot to remember, Bob.

BOB:
When the ground is colder than the air, and the air is below freezing, sometimes ice crystals will form on the ground.

This is called *hoarfrost*. Have you ever seen hoarfrost, Mr. Muffins?

MR. MUFFINS:
(Pause) Too easy, Bob.
How does snow sound?

BOB:
Sound?

MR. MUFFINS:
Yes. Let's talk about how it sounds.

BOB:
Well, a fresh, fluffy snowfall absorbs sound waves, so sometimes sounds we would normally hear are muffled. However, older snow, or snow that melts and refreezes and is therefore harder will reflect sound waves, making some sounds clearer. You may even be able to hear things from a greater distance because the surface of the snow acts like a megaphone.

MR. MUFFINS:
Where does it go?

BOB:
Where does what go, Mr. Muffins?

MR. MUFFINS:
You said the snow absorbs the sound. Where does the sound go when it is absorbed?

BOB:
No, I didn't mean—

MR. MUFFINS:
Does the snow keep the sound and then let it go later? Is that the sound the snow is making? Old sounds it held captive and now is letting loose?

BOB:
I'm not sure what you mean, Mr. Muffins. But...hey, kids, let's recap what we learned today, okay?

MR. MUFFINS:
You know, Antarctica has this waterfall that is formed from an underwater reservoir. The reservoir is super high in iron, and the iron oxidizes when it comes into contact with the air. Because of that, the waterfall is bright red. Do you know what the waterfall is called, Bob?

BOB:
I don't.

MR. MUFFINS:
I'll give you three guesses.

BOB:
I honestly don't know.

MR. MUFFINS:
That's one guess. (Slams head—the puppeteer's hand beneath the sock—against the countertop)

BOB:
Don't do that.

MR. MUFFINS:
That's number two. (Slams head even harder. A dark red stain leaks through fabric)

BOB:

I don't know!

MR. MUFFINS:

That's your last strike, Bob. Or should I say, my next strike. (Slams head against the counter. A distinct cracking sound is heard). Blood Falls! It's called Blood Falls! And the snow is pink there, too. (Hits head again, and again, and again, all while cackling hysterically)

BOB:

Jesus Christ! What the— (Reaches over to camera and turns it off. Feed stops)

Chapter Fourteen

As Rose watched from the window the previous afternoon, the calloused fingers of déjà vu slid jerkily along her spine.

She stood in the upstairs hall window, watching her daughter wrestle with the snow blower as the man across the street, Tom, pushed the snow from his front steps with the blade of his shovel. He wandered down to the sidewalk and began shoveling there when the man who lived next door appeared at the edge of his property.

Rose felt her face twist into a frown. Something wasn't right about the next-door neighbor. Rose had never met either man: she'd moved in with her daughter only the previous year, and Carol wasn't exactly a social butterfly. She only knew Tom's name from a passing mention from Carol at the dinner table, a throwaway comment about the couple across the street—Kim, was her name?—having two boys that attended Carol's school.

As she watched the neighbor approach Tom, dread inexplicably churned in Rose's stomach. It was the neighbor's mannerisms. There was something wooden about them, machine parts with gears that weren't quite lubricated enough to slide together smoothly. The neighbor's eyes fixed on Tom and did not move. Despite the frigid air and errant snowflakes sailing around his head, the man's eyes did not blink. Not once.

She had seen the same unnatural stare on another man, someone far back in her memory.

Rose was twenty-three when she married—almost an old maid, according to her mother. It was the early 1970s, though: women were finally making strides in achieving independence, and Rose was in no rush to settle down and raise a family. No, she wanted to travel the world. She graduated from Simmons College at twenty-two and landed a position as a bookkeeper for a high-end jewelry store on Boston's posh Newbury Street. One afternoon, as she exited the store to walk to the Common for lunch, a dark-haired man purchasing a bracelet for his mother's fiftieth birthday abandoned the sales counter to rush after her. When she did not turn at his verbal inquiries, he doubled his pace and placed a hand gently on her forearm.

Rose pulled away from his grasp and shrank back against the building. *Get away from me, you creep*, she signed.

Richard raised his hands like he was being held at gunpoint. "I'm so sorry," he said, embarrassed. "I—I didn't realize you couldn't hear me. I—"

That's a reason to put your hands on a stranger? Rose argued. *Didn't your mother teach you manners?*

"Wait," Richard pleaded. As he said it, he turned his hands so that his palms faced in, then wiggled his fingers. *She did, and I have no excuse*, he signed. *She is deaf, as well. I suppose I am used to touching her to get her attention. I saw you, and I...* He paused, his cheeks reddening. *You are the most beautiful woman I have ever seen, and I didn't want you to get away.*

Rose narrowed her eyes. *Get away? So women are like game? This is what your mother taught you?* She was still angry, but something about the man's vulnerability had softened her slightly.

Maybe, Richard signed, *you could come to dinner tonight at my parents' house and ask her yourself.*

Rose raised an eyebrow at him. Despite her best efforts, she felt a smile emerge on her face.

As it turned out, Richard's family owned the most successful travel agency chain in New England, and after they were married, Richard and Rose spent most of the first five years of their marriage touring the world, just as Rose had wanted. When they returned to Boston from abroad in February of 1978, their plane had difficulty landing. A storm front was arriving, one of the worst the city had seen in decades.

The snow doubled, then tripled in intensity as their cab left Logan Airport and headed down the expressway. "I'm sorry, Mister," said the driver, turning to the side and pushing down the hood on his bright red parka so that Richard could see the profile of his face. "It looks like the tunnel is closed. I have to head up toward Revere and take Route 1 back down."

Richard adjusted his hat and placed his hand on Rose's knee. "You gotta do what you gotta do," he said. They were in no hurry. *He has to take a detour,* Richard signed.

Rose nodded. *I just hope your father remembered to stop by the brownstone and turn on the heat.* She looked out the side window. Fistfuls of dime-sized flakes of white drifted by; they surrounded the cab in a menacing battalion. The atmosphere outside of the cab was more snow than air, and the prognosis for their journey worsened quickly. Traffic on the highway slowed to a crawl as the accumulation caused tires to slip and skid. Vehicles collided like bumper cars. Richard and Rose's cab passed a tractor-trailer stranded against the guardrail, its body jackknifed and blocking the breakdown and far right lanes.

Their driver leaned forward in his seat, trying to decipher the lane divisions. "I have to pull over," he said finally, and he eased the cab to the side of the highway. Nearly all of the cars had done the same, the depth of the snow quickly making travel physically impossible.

Richard craned his neck to try to see ahead of them. "How far is the off-ramp?" he asked. "Perhaps if you take one of the city roads—"

"It is at least a half mile away," the driver said. "The cab won't make it, and I wouldn't advise going on foot."

Richard turned to Rose. *We are going to be stuck here for a bit,* he signed. *There's nothing to worry about.*

She nodded at him.

A heavy truck roared by them, spitting gravel and slush against Richard's door. Richard began to roll down the window to clear it, but Rose placed a hand on his arm. She held her hands in front of her, palms facing down, crossed them, then pulled them apart. *Don't do that.*

Richard frowned. As he did so, the cab driver rolled his own window down. "Visibility is terrible," he said, sticking his head outside. A dusting of fresh snow fell over his head and onto his seat. Through the opening, Rose could see a line of cars parked along the other side of the highway, their occupants only fuzzy shadows smothered under thickening layers of white on their windows. The driver dipped his head further out of the vehicle. A moment later, he propped himself up and leaned his neck and shoulders outside as well. Finally, he ducked back inside, furiously rolled up the window, and turned to say something to Richard. Her husband nodded, and the driver got out of the car, closed the door, and stood next to the front of his car.

What is he doing? Rose asked, pointing at the road.

He said he needed to check something. Richard signed back. *Something he heard.* He placed his hands over Rose's and began to rub them, then signed again. *You must be cold.*

Your poor feet. They both looked down at Rose's slingback pumps. She had been wearing them on the plane because they were easy to kick off, but now she was regretting not wearing something more sensible. *Here. Let me keep them warm.* Richard leaned down and pulled Rose's shoes off. He wrapped both hands over her right foot and brought it up to his lap.

As Richard bent forward, however, the cab driver broke into a run. He sprinted across the highway toward a parked Buick, his bright red coat a laser pointer dot on a white screen. When he was only a few feet from the car, a lone pick-up truck making a valiant try to travel through the snow slid toward him. The driver, having spotted the cabbie, over-compensated and slammed on the brakes, causing the truck to rotate 45 degrees and hydroplane sideways, barreling toward the side of the road. Its hulking frame increased in speed as it streaked toward the cabbie, leaving him no place to escape. It pinned him against a nearby stationary vehicle with a muffled crunch.

Rose gasped and pointed at the truck. Richard signed, *What happened? What happened?* over and over, but Rose could only point, dumbstruck at what she had just witnessed. No one got out of their vehicle to check on the cab driver; even the man in the pick-up truck remained frozen behind the wheel.

Richard dropped Rose's foot and looked around, trying to gauge if the road was as treacherous as the driver had described. *Stay here,* he signed to his wife. When she raised a hand to stop him, Richard repeated his command, then kissed his wife firmly on the mouth. He pulled his hat down over his ears, opened his door, climbed out, then quickly climbed into the driver's seat. The keys were still in the ignition and Richard started the cab, pulled the gear shift into drive, and crept the car slowly forward. Carefully, Richard steered the cab around the parked cars in front of them and began to pull away.

Rose looked at the pick-up truck, its front end collapsed and melded into the Buick's rear quadrant. A piece of bright red fabric stained with dark liquid was visible where the two vehicles joined. Richard kept his eyes facing forward, trying to discern what lay before them between gray streaks of the windshield wiper.

And then.

Next to her, just outside of her window, he appeared, jogging alongside the cab: a marathon runner training for his next race. The cab driver, with the hood of his bright red parka pulled tightly atop his head, kept pace with them, his eyes fixed on Richard as he inched the car through mounds of snow and slush piling up along the highway. Rose wiped her fingers across the condensation on the glass and looked at him. The cab driver did not blink. Snow poured from the sky onto his face. It slipped between his slightly parted lips. It landed on his eyeballs and melted into them, and still, the driver did not blink. *Go, Richard!* Rose thought. *Go! Go go go go!* She willed her husband to make the cab move faster, but he maintained the same methodical pace.

Slow and steady wins the race, she thought. A tortoise at the mercy of the hare.

Finally, it was there: the exit ramp. Excitedly, Richard steered the cab to the right. The wheels revolted and shimmied the car's rear end to the left, but Richard turned the steering wheel counterclockwise and the car righted itself again. They crept down the ramp and onto the street below. Richard turned left and parked the cab under the overpass, and leaving the engine running, returned to the back seat of the cab, wrapping his arms around his wife and hugging her to him.

His chest vibrated, and she knew what he was saying to her without seeing his lips move. *I love you. I love you.*

Rose kept her eyes peeled out of the back window, at the off-ramp. The cab driver was nowhere to be seen.

* * *

Nearly a half-century later, Rose's neighbor had the same eyes as the cab driver as he walked toward Tom. Tom, in turn, stopped shoveling the sidewalk and greeted him. When they were within a few feet of one another, the neighbor began to speak. He spoke for a long time—more than a full minute, at Rose's estimation, though Rose could not discern what he was saying. As he did so, Tom removed his winter hat and squeezed it hard in his hands as if palpitating it. He stared intensely at his neighbor as he rattled on until, when a lapse in the conversation appeared to occur, he wrenched his hat back onto his head, folding the bottom edge upward so that the back of his neck and his ears were exposed. As he did so, the neighbor leaned forward and said something directly into Tom's right ear, something that made the latter jump back as if in repulsion. Tom looked long and hard at the neighbor, the two saying nothing for a long moment, until Tom picked up his snow shovel and walked slowly down the sidewalk, past the border of his own front yard and toward the next house's driveway.

An enormous plow rumbled down the road, dropping its big silver blade onto the snow and pushing tall piles of the heavy white mess onto and over the curb. Rose could see the driver bobbing his head groggily behind a windshield dotted with weather debris.

Tom took a sharp left, turning not into his neighbor's walk but toward the street. Even as his feet sank deep into the heavy blanket of undisturbed white, he did not slow. Instead, he maintained a steady pace through the snow, into the road, and directly in front of the oncoming plow. It happened so quickly, Rose did not have time to look away.

As the plow's blade touched Tom's boots, it did not push him but instead swept him up, a sly soccer half-back performing the perfect slide tackle. The bright blue hat fell from his head as Tom sailed backward and seemed to float, if only for a moment, atop a fast-moving cloud of snow and ice. Then, as quickly as he'd been scooped up by the vehicle, the rotation of the frozen refuse in front of the blade churned and folded his body into its mix, pulling inside first one arm, then his torso and legs, until finally, his head disappeared under the motile pile. The blade bucked slightly, a motion echoed soon after by the body of the truck as if passing over a large speed bump too quickly.

The driver made no motion to stop, and as the truck sailed past Carol and Rose's house and down the road, a viscous ooze of red and brown smeared along the ground behind it, the tall wall of snow pushed along the margin of the street displaying hints of Tom's mangled body in winks and peeks. A shoe protruded here, a glove there, the final inkling of Tom sitting on top of the pile two houses down as the bright blue wool glimmered in the dying sunlight beneath a smudge of flesh that resembled Tom's salt and pepper sideburn and an ear.

A flash of orange from in front of her house drew Rose's attention. She looked down to see a fat ginger-colored cat leap through the snow toward the path Carol cleared on the sidewalk. Her daughter did not see the animal and seemed lost in her own thoughts as she pushed the blower toward the neighbor's driveway. Rose waved her arms to try to get the cat's attention; she didn't want it sucked up by the machine. It did not appear to register her movement in the upstairs window, but Carol glanced up and offered a hesitant wave toward her mother, her eyes and mouth registering confusion.

Quickly, Rose hobbled down the carpeted stairs and stepped into her boots. She wrapped her coat around her shoulders and scurried outside, hoping she wasn't too late. A blur of orange raced by her and into the backyard, and Rose attempted to follow, plunging her feet into the knee-high snow by the fence and leaning down to try to spy the animal who seemed to have been swallowed by the drifts. The wind was more aggressive than it had been the previous day, and it swept snow into her face and blew the hood away from her head.

Suddenly, a firm hand grasped her by the shoulder and spun her around. Carol, her face twisted in a grotesque fit of anger, began to scream in her face. Her breath blew hot clouds of fog onto Rose's cheeks. Carol shook Rose so violently, Rose could not focus on her daughter's lips to discern what she was saying, but the cat—

Carol stopped yelling. She stopped shaking and moved her hands down to Rose's wrists and held them, softly.

Rose pointed to the back of the yard, tried to explain that she was worried about the orange cat, but Carol wanted none of it. Tears streamed down the daughter's face even as she did not seem to notice them. Rose glanced back at the shed. There was no sign of the cat, not even a half-hearted path where the creature may have burrowed.

Please. Carol signed, letting go of her mother's arms. *It's too cold out for you to be out here.*

Rose exhaled slowly. She nodded, then took her daughter's hand and held it. The soft fabric of the glove felt good against her cold fingers. She let Carol lead her back to the house. As the two carefully climbed the steps to the small entranceway off the kitchen, Rose took one last look across the street.

There stood the neighbor, the one who had spoken to Tom just before he walked in front of the speeding plow. He stared at Rose, his eyes unblinking. The more she looked at him, the more Rose realized: the person standing across the street was not the neighbor at all. As she watched, his face began to contort and shift; his features stretched and bubbled until the topography of his face shuffled and realigned into that of the sandy-haired bartender who lived two houses down. The landscape of his face scrambled again, and then, he was neither the neighbor nor the bartender. He was Tom.

Rose glanced at the pile of snow several houses down on the perimeter of the road. The bright blue hat was there, and yet, it was also on Tom, on the figure who resembled Tom, on the strange shape-shifter who walked calmly back up his driveway and into his house, just as Rose's daughter, Carol, ventured back outside and into the cold.

Chapter Fifteen

W indy Weather's dress was yellow on Thursday morning's newscast, but it was just as form-fitting as the red one had been. "...as Massachusetts residents dig themselves out from this Winter Storm Mia, it looks like we'll have another headache to contend with: possible flooding over portions of the Valley, especially along the Connecticut River." She waved her hand down the green-screened map, then punctuated her statement with an awkward smile.

John Stephenson lay on his sofa, a thick blanket curled around his body, and watched Windy with mild interest. "Temperatures will climb to the mid-40s by the afternoon, bringing with them some heavy rain," she continued. John dipped his head toward the window and looked out at the sky. Sure enough, a cabal of dark clouds huddled in a conspiracy to the west. "Fifteen degrees colder, and we'd be looking at a foot more of accumulation, but this front will have the opposite effect: most of that freshly packed powder will be washed away by the weekend. Make sure you clear those storm drains and—"

A loud thundering echoed from the side of his house.

John pushed the coverlet from his pajamas and stood up. It was early yet—most of his neighbors hadn't left for work, he knew—so the cacophony was all the more disconcerting. He stepped into his sneakers and walked onto the porch. A large plow pushed pile after pile of snow from his driveway onto his front lawn. A second man pushed a hand plow down his sidewalk, blowing the remnants carelessly onto the street. John waved at the man behind the wheel and the driver gave him a half-hearted gesture back. His face was drawn and weary; he had likely worked all of the previous night.

This was a relief. He wasn't going to starve to death, John thought. His rotting corpse would not be eaten by—Wait. John saw something orange run across the layer of packed snow crusted along the street. He moved closer to the screen door and tried to peer past the plow truck. Sure enough, Jonesy the cat scuttled across the road again, running straight for John's front lawn and headlong toward the door: Headlong toward the back wheels of the plow truck and directly in front of the rotating blades of the manual snow blower.

John did not stop to think. He pushed open the door and ran toward the man pushing the blower. As he did, the worker paused, a confused look in his eyes, and glanced down at the controls to shut the machine off. Jonesy continued his run onto the front lawn, where John jumped into the cat's path and sprawled across the ground, trapping the cat with his body, a makeshift net.

Around the two of them, the world spun. The sky tilted on its axis and a fistful of adrenaline shoved itself down John's throat. Each breath grew shallower, but John remained curled tightly around the cat even as he fought to force his diaphragm to unlock. It was getting harder to breathe.

The man driving the truck opened his door and stuck his head outside. "Hey, you okay?" he yelled half-heartedly.

John nodded his head, unsure if the man could see him. If he hadn't, he still closed his door and backed the truck out into the street. His assistant rolled the snow blower onto the truck bed and jumped into the passenger seat, and within two minutes of John making his first appearance outside in more than half a decade, the two men were gone.

"I think you can let him up now," said a voice from behind John.

John lifted his head and looked toward the driveway. Louis stood by the edge of the steps, his hands resting on his hips. "Did the landscaping guys come by and clear the driveway this morning?" he asked, looking around at the nearly naked blacktop.

John sat up. The orange cat glanced up at him, then collapsed onto his side, twisting his body playfully in the snow. "Yeah," said John hesitantly. "Didn't you see them leave just now?"

Louis looked around, then back at John. He shrugged. "I was at Jackie's." He pointed next door. "That's where I parked. I went to turn into the driveway here, but it wasn't clear." He shifted from one foot to the other uncomfortably. "I'm sorry. I should have checked in on you earlier."

John smiled, trying to appear nonchalant. He reached down to Jonesy and gently petted his fur. "It's okay. I need to learn to do things for myself."

"You seem to be getting along all right on that front."

John cautiously looked around. A wave of white-knuckle anxiety somersaulted over him, and he closed his eyes and begged it to be on its way. "Hey, look at me," he said weakly. "I'm outside."

"So you are."

The two were silent for a long minute. Jonesy rolled over and hopped back onto his feet. He paused and sniffed John's hand, then walked purposefully toward the porch. Without a word, Louis opened the screen door and let the cat inside.

"I missed you, Louis," John said finally. "I really missed you."

Louis smiled and walked over to John, still sitting in the snow in his night clothes and sneakers. John looked up at Louis. His ex's mouth was frozen in an unsettling grin; his pupils were wide and dark. He stared back at John, unblinking.

Then, Louis bent down and whispered into John's ear, the icy chill of his breath making small clouds of smoke along John's jawbone.

From the sky came the first trickles of rain.

"A Great White Hurricane Blankets the City"

The New York Daily News
March 15, 1888

The frozen bodies of more than one hundred residents of the five boroughs have been discovered in various places around the city, some buried within snowbanks, others out in the open. Exposure seems to have claimed many of the unfortunate, but for others, the cause of death remains unknown.

Although the skies did not hint at anything more than a passing rainstorm, by nightfall on Sunday, temperatures plummeted, and at Monday morning's sunrise, fifteen inches of heavy snow had blanketed the city. The storm, boasting gales up to eighty miles per hour at times, continued throughout the next two days, only tapering in the wee hours of Wednesday, leaving the country's largest metropolis buried beneath more than fifty inches of tightly packed powder and ice.

Intrepid policemen patrolled the area, aiding the occasional hapless pedestrian and funneling transients toward the nearest station where they might safely bunk in the hallways for the night. One such officer was spotted marching up Sixth Avenue in the heart of the blizzard, at one point stopping, then crouching down into the drifts swirling about him. According to one onlooker, the man removed his hat and scarf and turned an ear toward the brutal wind as if straining to hear something. A cry for help, perhaps? Tragically, his body was later discovered next to a comfort station at the east end of Bryant Park (formerly Reservoir Square), curled up in a fetal position but staring blankly into the sky.

The storm rendered the Brooklyn Bridge impassable, leaving borough residents stranded, unable to return to their families until a series of ice dams floated down the East River and became stuck to the base of the bridge, creating a makeshift passage. While authorities cautioned that the temporary corridor was unsafe, a number of bold men steeled their gait to cross. One undaunted gentleman leaped onto the ice promenade just as it disassembled, sending him sailing toward the Atlantic on the frozen raft, eventually crashing into Governors Island where, instead of climbing to safety, the man inexplicably dove into the glacial water, never to resurface.

Electric streetlights were rendered inoperable and the city did not light gas lamps, leaving the nighttime streets dark as coal while the maelstrom thundered on. Telegraph poles toppled and wires became tangled in the hooves of startled horses, cutting off all communication to neighboring cities.

The Great Blizzard of 1888 lasted all of two and a half days, but as more remains are unearthed from the frozen deluge, authorities contend with piecing together what exactly occurred over the past sixty hours.

A gentleman working for Thomas Edison is being interviewed after police detained him on the train back to Menlo Park once transportation was restored. He claims to have captured the sound of the storm for posterity, imprinting its noise onto one of his boss's phonographs.

His reason for doing so is yet unknown.

Acknowledgments

They say it takes a village to raise a child. It took a neighborhood (snowy and otherwise) to build this book, and for that, I send my sincere gratitude...to Dylan Burakiewicz and Aaron Fay, my go-to guys with any questions I have about music terminology. Those ear worms I dropped inside your brain? They are the ones who dug them from the ground with me. To Anthony Santiago, the anatomy expert who, for the past decade, has answered my questions about the best ways to kill people (but never once has asked if it's for a story) and to Ralfi Viviano and Mariah McNamara, the forensics experts who aided me with delineating the gruesome details of postmortem examinations. To Louis Stephenson, who helped shovel the walk and reveal a path, to everyone at CLASH who welcomed the storm, and to Becky LeJeune, who pushed my ass into the sled and kept it there. To my intrepid students from the class of 2024 who requested to be namesakes in this book, no matter what degree of gruesomeness the plot imparted, and as always, to Ruth Estabrook, Melissa Mumby, and Zachary Hastings-Hooper, who routinely buy my ramblings and read them... and like me anyway.

Above all, thank you, Izabela Ziobro. You got those boys off my lawn. Rest in peace.

Rebecca Rowland
A frigid weekend in April 2025
Western Massachusetts

About the Author

Rebecca Rowland is a Shirley Jackson and Bram Stoker Award finalist. *Cemetery Dance* stated that her fiction "reeks of *The Twilight Zone* in all the best ways." Despite her love of the ocean and distaste for cold weather, Rebecca makes her home in a landlocked and often icy corner of New England (USA). She is represented by CW Literary. For more information, follow her on Instagram at Rebecca_Rowland_books or visit RowlandBooks.com.

Also by CLASH Books

BLACK BRANE

Michael Cisco

8114

Joshua Hull

THE MIDNIGHT MUSE

Jo Kaplan

EVERYTHING THE DARKNESS EATS

Eric LaRocca

STRANGE STONES

Edward Lee & Mary SanGiovanni

A PLAY ABOUT A CURSE

Caroline Macon Fleischer

ON SUBMISSION

Michael J. Seidlinger

BELOW THE GRAND HOTEL

Cat Scully

I CAN FIX HER

Rae Wilde

OF BEASTS

M. Jane Worma